"Rick? W Here?" Joanna Asked.

The desire to kiss her was almost overpowering to Rick. But it was at odds with the renewed feeling of betrayal that seared through him. She obviously had moved on with her life and was now carrying some other man's child.

"Are you all right?" he asked, his voice harsh with anger, with hurt.

She started to say something and had her breath stolen away before she could utter an intelligible sound. Her eyes widened as her hand flew to her abdomen.

"What's the matter?" On his knees beside her, concern pushed aside his anger.

"The baby," Joanna gasped, pushing the words out as best she could. "I think the baby's coming."

"You mean later."

"I mean *now*." Joanna clenched his wrist.

"Hold on," Rick told her, beginning to rise to his feet. "I'll go get help." The death grip tightened on his wrist, yanking him back down to her.

"Rick, you *are* help."

Dear Reader,

Spring into the new season with six fresh passionate, powerful and provocative love stories from Silhouette Desire.

Experience first love with a young nurse and the arrogant surgeon who stole her innocence, in *USA TODAY* bestselling author Elizabeth Bevarly's *Taming the Beastly MD* (#1501), the latest title in the riveting DYNASTIES: THE BARONES continuity series. Another *USA TODAY* bestselling author, Cait London, offers a second title in her HEARTBREAKERS miniseries—*Instinctive Male* (#1502) is the story of a vulnerable heiress who finds love in the arms of an autocratic tycoon.

And don't miss RITA® Award winner Marie Ferrarella's *A Bachelor and a Baby* (#1503), the second book of Silhouette's crossline series THE MOM SQUAD, featuring single mothers who find true love. In *Tycoon for Auction* (#1504) by Katherine Garbera, a lady executive wins the services of a commitment-shy bachelor. A playboy falls in love with his secretary in *Billionaire Boss* (#1505) by Meagan McKinney, the latest MATCHED IN MONTANA title. And a Native American hero's fling with a summer-school teacher produces unexpected complications in *Warrior in Her Bed* (#1506) by Cathleen Galitz.

This April, shower yourself with all six of these moving and sensual new love stories from Silhouette Desire.

Enjoy!

Joan Marlow Golan

Joan Marlow Golan
Senior Editor, Silhouette Desire

Please address questions and book requests to:
Silhouette Reader Service
U.S.: 3010 Walden Ave., P.O. Box 1325, Buffalo, NY 14269
Canadian: P.O. Box 609, Fort Erie, Ont. L2A 5X3

A Bachelor
and a Baby
MARIE FERRARELLA

Published by Silhouette Books
America's Publisher of Contemporary Romance

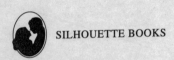

SILHOUETTE BOOKS

ISBN 0-373-76503-7

A BACHELOR AND A BABY

Printed in U.S.A.

Books by Marie Ferrarella in Miniseries

MARIE FERRARELLA

earned a master's degree in Shakespearean comedy and, perhaps as a result, her writing is distinguished by humor and natural dialogue. This RITA® Award-winning author's goal is to entertain and to make people laugh and feel good. She has written over one hundred books for Silhouette, some under the name Marie Nicole. Her romances are beloved by fans worldwide and have been translated into Spanish, Italian, German, Russian, Polish, Japanese and Korean.

To
Joan Marlow Golan,
with thanks
for the homecoming

One

Rick Masters wasn't given to cruising around in his car. Certainly not in what was considered to be well past the shank of the evening.

It wasn't as if he was at loose ends with nothing to do. A stack of reports waited for his perusal, a pile of documents needed his signature and hundreds of people had lives on the cusp of being rearranged, all on his say-so once he made up his mind about the relocation of the present corporate headquarters for Masters Enterprises.

This wasn't the time to be driving around aimlessly on deserted streets.

Well, not aimlessly.

He hadn't been aimless in a very long time. And no matter what he tried to tell himself, he knew exactly where he was going. He'd finally given in and looked her up in the telephone book an hour ago.

She still lived there. In the old house. The one he still dreamed about on balmy nights when his mind gave him no peace.

Like tonight.

Maybe it was a mistake, coming back. Maybe this was the one challenge he should have turned his back on.

Too late now.

Besides, leaving a question unanswered was too much like letting the challenge win. Ever since he could walk, he'd always been too competitive to allow that to happen.

He'd taken that light a little too fast. Rick raised his dark eyes to look in the rearview mirror. No dancing blue and red lights approached.

He had to be careful, he told himself. There was no sense in letting his emotions run away with him, stealing away his tendency to be careful.

The way they once had, leading him down a path where he was vulnerable.

It seemed like a million years ago.

It seemed like yesterday.

He glanced along the silent, sleeping streets where he had grown up. It felt strange, being back. Stranger still to know that she still lived here in Bedford. When he'd left, he'd purposely never asked about her. Never given in to his curiosity about just what path her life had taken. It was enough that it was away from him.

Out of sight was supposed to be out of mind.

Right now, the only thing that appeared to be out of mind was him, he thought. Ironic amusement curved his generous mouth as he turned right at the next corner. There was a shopping mall now. He could remember when it was just an orange grove.

Bedford had done a lot of growing up in the last eight years. Why not? He had.

And yet, had he? Part of him didn't feel like the successful VP of Masters Enterprises. Part of him still felt like that young boy, head over heels in love with the wrong person. Except that then, he hadn't thought she was the wrong person.

But he had learned.

Learned a lot of things. Mostly how to take the helm of his father's company. He'd gotten to his present position on merit, not by coasting there because he was the boss's son. If he'd coasted, no way would he have been able to take over operations after his father's heart attack last October. The transition in management from father to son in the last six months had been an incredibly smooth one. And why not? All he did was live and breathe business these days. There was nothing else for him, not since he'd been betrayed by the last person in the world he would have thought capable of it.

Served him right for leading with his heart rather than his head. First and last time. It wasn't as if he hadn't been warned. Both his parents had told him that someone in his position had to be careful about the friends he made, the women he cared for.

Well, he'd learned all right. The lessons that you paid for dearly in life were the ones that stuck.

So what was he doing driving through her part of town, driving onto the winding streets of her development, threading his way toward her block?

He really didn't know.

He didn't turn back.

Self-torture had never been his way. He'd always been the philosophical one. Things happened. You got over them and moved on. And he had. Moved all the way across country to Atlanta, Georgia, the place that, until a month ago, had been the headquarters of his father's company. Georgia, where his grandfather had originally been from. But certain economical circumstances had arisen in the last year that made that arrangement no longer as advantageous as it once had been. Almost fully recovered from his heart attack, Howard Masters wanted to have the home office of his company moved to Southern California so that he could be closer to its operations. Tax advantages were no longer a factor. Only control was.

The old man still wanted to exercise control over the company his great-grandfather had begun in the back of a barn. Rick couldn't fault him. Keeping control had something to do with extending a man's mortality and Rick could sympathize with that.

Even so, he'd resisted the move at first. But then, he'd challenged himself to face up to his demons. After all, he'd been in love with Joanna a long time ago. He was smart enough now to know that love wasn't something to build a life on.

If he doubted that, he had only to look to his parents. Two icons of the social world who'd looked perfect together on paper, in photographs, everywhere but in real life.

Love, that wild, heady mysterious substance he'd once believed to have taken command of his soul, was only the stuff they wrote songs about. It had no place in the real world, and he was part of the real world.

What he did or didn't do affected thousands of people. Heavy burden, that.

He should be turning back. It was late and he had things to do.

The April night was crisp and clear and unusually warm, even for Southern California. He'd left the windows of his classic 64 Mustang down. His father had urged him to get a car more suitable to his present station, so he drove a Mercedes to work, but he'd refused to get rid of his Mustang. He wanted the car. Even though it had been the one he'd been driving the night he'd wanted to elope with Joanna. Even though they had made love in that car.

Or maybe because of it.

Rick shook his head as he retraced his way through a maze of ever-climbing streets. Hell of a time to be playing shrink with himself.

The houses here all lined one side of the street, their faces looking out onto carefully manicured vegetation that hid the backs of other houses as they progressed up the hill.

One more block and then he'd be passing her house.

Dumb idea, Rick upbraided himself. He needed to be getting back. Those contracts weren't going to review themselves and he believed in being a hands-on executive.

Hands. He could remember the way his hands had felt on her warm, supple flesh, remembered how it felt to lay her down on the cool spring grass and make love with her in the meadow behind his parents' summer home. It was just the two of them there. The two of them against the world.

Until he discovered what she was really like.

Rick wrinkled his nose. An acrid smell wove its way into the stillness.

Probably just someone using their fireplace. Some people didn't care if it was warm or not. It was just the beginning of spring and a fire in the fireplace was romantic.

His mind started to drift back again, remembering.

He knew he shouldn't have come this far. Annoyed with himself, Rick looked around for some place to turn his car around and go back the way he'd come.

The smell didn't go away.

Instead, it intensified with each passing second. He wasn't sure exactly what made him push on instead of turn around, but he kept going.

Like someone hypnotized, he pressed his foot down on the accelerator, urging his car up the incline and toward the smell.

And then he saw it.

The sky was filled with black smoke.

Joanna felt herself rebelling.

The dream was back to haunt her. The one where everything and everyone was obscured. The one that had her running barefoot, in her nightgown, through an open field enshrouded in fog and mists.

Everything was hidden from her. Hidden and threatening.

But this time, it wasn't fog, it was smoke that curled around her legs and crept stealthily along her body.

It didn't matter, the effect was the same.

She was lost, so very lost. And then she began

running faster, desperately searching for a way out. Looking for someone to help her.

There was no one.

She was alone.

Every time she thought she could make out a shape, a person, they would disappear as she ran toward them. The resulting emptiness mocked her.

It was a dream, just a dream, she told herself over and over again as she ran. Her heart twisted within her, aching in its loneliness.

She'd be all right if she could just open her eyes. Just bridge her way back into the real world. Over and over again, she told herself to wake up.

With superhuman effort, she forced open her eyes.

They began to smart.

Joanna woke up choking. Her lungs began to ache. Had the nightmare taken on another dimension? Groggy, she sat up in bed. Her bulk prevented her from making the transition from lying to sitting an easy one. She felt as if she'd been pregnant since the beginning of time instead of almost nine months.

Your own fault. You asked for this.

Her eyes were seriously tearing now. This wasn't part of her dream. She smelled smoke, felt heat even though she'd shut the heat off just before she'd gone to bed more than an hour ago.

And then she realized what was happening. Her house was on fire.

Stunned, her heart pounding as she scrambled out of bed, Joanna grabbed the long robe that was slung over the footboard. She was hardly aware of jamming her fists through the sleeves.

Barefoot, Joanna hurried to her bedroom doorway,

only to see that her living room was flooded in smoke. A line of fire had shadowed her steps, racing in front of her. It was now feeding on the door frame, preventing her flight.

Flames shot up all around her.

Something came crashing down right in front of her, barely missing her. Backing up, she screamed as flames leaped to the bottom of her robe, eating away at the hem. Working frantically, Joanna shed the robe before the flames could find her.

Driving quickly, Rick took the next corner at a speed that almost made the Mustang tip over. He jerked his cell phone out of his pocket and hit 911 on the keypad with his thumb.

The instant the dispatch came in the line, he snapped out his location, adding, "Two houses are on fire, one's almost gone."

As the woman asked him to repeat what he'd just said, he heard someone scream from within Joanna's house. Rick tossed the phone aside. It landed on the passenger seat as he bolted from the car. He barely remembered to cut off the engine.

The scream echoed in his brain.

Somehow he knew it wasn't her mother, wasn't some renter or some trick of the imagination.

That was Joanna's scream.

She was in there, in that inferno. And he had to get her out.

The last house on the corner, next to Joanna's, was already engulfed in flames. It looked as if the fire had started there and had spread to Joanna's house. So far, from what he could see as he ran toward the building, only the rear portion was burning.

That was where the bedrooms were, he remembered. And she was in one of them.

Racing to the front door, he twisted the knob. It was locked and there was no way he could jimmy it open. His talents didn't run in those directions. But he could think on his feet.

Stripping off his jacket, Rick wrapped it around his arm and swung at the front window as hard as he could. Glass shattered, raining down in chunks. Moving quickly, Rick cleared away as much as he could then let himself into the house.

He stopped only long enough to unlock the front door. He left it open, a portal to the outside world. He had a feeling he was going to need that to guide him out. Inside, the inferno grew.

"Joanna!" Cupping his mouth, he yelled again. "Joanna, where are you?"

The flames had momentarily frozen her in place as her mind raced on alternative routes of escape, trying to assimilate what was going on.

Was she dreaming?

She had to be. Why else would she be hearing Rick's voice calling to her? Rick was gone. Had been gone for eight years.

Without a word to her.

Maybe she was already dead. Maybe the smoke had gotten to her and she was having some kind of out-of-body experience.

A fireman. It had to be a fireman. She only thought it sounded like Rick.

"Here," she screamed. "I'm in here." Smoke crowded its way into her throat, slashing at her words, sucking away her breath. "In the back bedroom." Eyes smarting, she couldn't make out the doorway anymore. "I can't get out. Help me!"

Like a behemoth, the fire snarled and groaned, playing tricks on his ears, his eyes. He was sure he heard her, heard her voice, muffled but still strong, calling out. Flames belched out of the rear of the house now.

Despite the temperature, his blood turned cold in his veins.

Think, damn it, think.

And then an idea came to him. Running to the kitchen, he passed through the dining room. Rick stopped only long enough to grab the tablecloth and yank it off the table. He soaked the entire cloth in the sink, then hurried with it to the rear of the house.

Toward the sound of her voice.

There were curtains of fire everywhere. He couldn't see more than a foot in front of him. "Joanna? Joanna where are you?"

"Here, I'm here," Joanna called out. She couldn't get out the door and when she ran toward the window, she found her way blocked there as well. There was no way to get to the window. The rug beneath her feet was burning.

And then suddenly, something came rolling in on the floor, crashing through the flames. As she stared, the figure took shape, rising up to assume the full height of a man.

The room began to spin. She thought she saw Rick

Masters, her tablecloth wrapped around his head and shoulders, reaching out to her.

The next moment, she felt herself being wrapped up in the tablecloth. He was pressing it to her face, over her mouth. It was dripping wet. Joanna tried to drag in air and only felt smoke clogging her lungs.

"Let's go!"

The order echoed in her head, sounding so like Rick. She was going to die in some stranger's arms, remembering Rick.

The man's arms were around her as he urged her blindly on through what felt like an entire wall of fire.

Joanna tried to protest that she couldn't make it, but the words never rose to her lips. The man who looked like Rick was pushing her.

She felt herself stumbling. Falling.

The next moment, she felt his arms encircling her. And then suddenly, she was airborne. He was carrying her, carrying her through the inferno.

The heat was everywhere. She could hear it, feel it. And there was pain everywhere as well. Pain that was radiating not from the outside, but from within.

Something was tearing her in two.

Joanna bit down on her lip, but the scream came anyway. It shook her body, traveling down toward the center, toward the source of the pain. The pain wouldn't stop.

And then suddenly, the heat was gone.

She was being lowered.

Grass, there was grass beneath her.

Desperate, Joanna clawed her way out of the singed fabric enclosure that was still over her head and face.

And then it was off, lying in a heap on the ground next to her.

Gulping in air, Joanna looked around frantically, trying to get her bearings, trying to clear her head of the hallucination that insisted on sticking to her like a second skin.

She blinked several times, but the man sitting on the front lawn beside her, panting, with the smell of smoke clinging to every surface of his body, didn't resume his shape.

Didn't transform from who she thought she saw to who he really was.

He stayed the same.

Was she dead? Was that it? Was that why she was still staring up at Rick Masters?

There didn't seem to be any other possible explanation for it.

Rick dragged air back into his lungs. The house next to Joanna's was encased in flames. He saw no signs of anyone having escaped. His legs shook as he rose to his feet. He felt her grab his arm, pulling him back.

He looked at her over his shoulder. "Let go, I've got to see if I can get anyone out."

"There's no one there," she gasped out. "They're away on vacation." Her eyes still burned and she squeezed them shut for a moment, then opened them again. He was still there.

"How about in your house?"

She thought she shook her head. She wasn't sure if she did or not. "Nobody."

Rick sank down on the ground again. His heart was

slamming madly against his chest. "Are you all right?" he demanded.

He sounded angry. They hadn't seen one another in eight years and he sounded angry. Why? If anything, she should have been the one who was angry. Angry because he hadn't come after her the way she'd hoped, prayed that he would.

But he couldn't be here. Could he? Was she losing her mind?

Shaken, her head spinning, she stared at him, still afraid to believe that she wasn't somehow hallucinating all this.

"Rick? What are you doing here?"

The desire to hold her in his arms, to kiss her and make the world back off, was almost overpowering. But it was at odds with the renewed feeling of betrayal that seared through him. He might not have moved on with his life in the full sense of the word, but she obviously had. Moved on, married and was now carrying some other man's child in her body.

The sting he felt was unbelievably sharp and deep. Though he'd never talked about it, he'd thought of having children with her. Lots of children. Children with her face and his sense of logic.

Damn it, Joey, why did you do this to me?

"I asked you a question," he said his voice harsh with anger, with hurt. "Are you all right?"

Her mouth fell open. She wasn't dead. She was alive. And he was real. He was here. After all this time, he was here. Looking at her the way she never wanted him to look at her. She'd walked out of his life just to avoid that look in his eyes.

And yet, after all this time, here he was, looking at her as if he hated her.

She started to say something, and had her breath stolen away before she could utter an intelligible sound. What came out of her mouth was a purely guttural cry.

Joanna's eyes widened as her hand flew to her abdomen. The pain she'd been peripherally conscious of intensified, pushing itself to center stage and demanding attention.

"What? What's the matter?" On his knees beside her, concern pushed aside his anger.

Rick strained to hear the sound of sirens approaching, but there was nothing. Not only that, but there didn't appear to be any activity, or even any lights being turned on from the three other houses on the immediate block.

Where the hell was everyone? Had he and Joanna just slipped into some private twilight zone of their own?

Joanna clutched his arm, her nails digging into his flesh, her face drained of all color. She wasn't answering his question.

This couldn't be happening, she thought, frantically Not now. She wasn't due for another two weeks. The doctor had promised her.

Promises were meant to be broken.

The promise between her and Rick had been.

"The baby," she gasped, pushing the words out as best she could. "I think the baby's coming."

Two

___

Dumbfounded, Rick could only stare at her. "You mean later."

She couldn't be saying what he thought she was saying. Rick looked from her face to her abdomen and then back at her face again. That had to be the panic talking, he decided.

Joanna could almost feel her knuckles breaking out through her skin as she clenched his wrist.

"I mean *now.*" The word rode out on a torrent of pain.

Crouching beside her, Rick carefully peeled her fingers from his wrist. She'd almost cut off his circulation. "Hang on, the paramedics have got to be getting here soon."

Instinctively she knew that they'd never make it in time.

Joanna shook her head violently from side to side, the pain all but cracking her in half. "Unless they're invisible and already here...they're going to be too late." She looked up at him. God, but life was strange, bringing them together like this, now of all times. "You're going to have to help me."

There were a great many things he'd learned how to do, felt comfortable in undertaking. Delivering a baby was not one of them. "Me?"

Even with the throbbing sound echoing in her head, Joanna could hear the wariness in Rick's voice. She couldn't very well blame him. This wasn't exactly her idea of ideal circumstances, either.

"I don't...like this any better...than...you do, but this baby...is coming...and I need...someone...on the other end." It was getting more and more difficult for her to talk, to frame complete thoughts. The pain kept snatching away her breath, railroading her mind. Panic was attempting to push its way into her consciousness.

Desperate, Rick looked over his shoulder at the other three houses on the block. They were all dark. Why hadn't any lights gone on? Why wasn't anyone home?

Where the hell *was* everyone?

Where they were didn't matter. What did matter was that he was here and so was she. And she needed him.

It occurred to him that for the second time in his life, he hadn't the slightest idea what to do. And both times had involved Joanna.

Someone had to be home on the next block. "Hold

on,'' he told her, beginning to rise to his feet. ''I'll
go get help.''

The death grip tightened on his wrist, yanking him
back down to her with a strength he didn't think she
was capable of.

''You *are* help...'' She raised her eyes to his.
''Please.''

Damn it, she still knew just how to rip into his
heart. Even after all this time. Rick knew he had no
choice.

''Okay. I—'' He saw her jerk and stiffen, her eyes
opening so wide, they looked as if they could fall out
at any moment.

Joanna bit down on her lip so hard, she thought she
tasted blood. A scream welled up in her throat, its
magnitude nearly matching the agony assaulting her.
It felt as if she were a holiday turkey and someone
had taken a buzz saw to her body.

''I have to push...I have to push...I have to push.''
The words came out in a frantic rush.

He knew next to nothing about what was involved
in delivering a baby, but it had to take longer than
this. She had to be wrong. ''Are you sure?''

Clutching his hand as if it were her very lifeline,
Joanna managed to pull herself up into a semi-sitting
position. ''I'm sure...oh God...I'm sure.'' How did
someone feel like this and still live?

Fear gnawed at her. Belatedly, recalling something
Lori had said to the Lamaze class about not being
able to pant and push at the same time, Joanna began
panting hard. Praying that the action would at least
temporarily divert this overwhelming urge she had to
push the baby out.

Nothing she'd read or heard had prepared her for the reality of this. Before she'd ever walked into the sperm bank, she had read about every possible scenario that could happen at this juncture.

Every bad one now flashed before her, stealing away her courage.

She'd been so sure about this. So sure. She hadn't even regretted her decision when the local school board had tactfully "suggested" that she take an unpaid leave of absence until after her baby was born. Since she was a high-school English teacher, her condition in the somewhat conservative town was a source of discomfort and embarrassment to a number of the parents. But even then, she'd been sure about her choice to go this route alone.

Now she wasn't sure about being alone or even the route itself. Now there was only a sense of panic tearing into her with steel claws.

Here she was, her house in flames, her life in shambles, giving birth to a fatherless baby on the front lawn with the only man she'd ever loved inexplicably standing over her.

She felt as if she'd lost her grasp on reality.

"Ricky...I'm...scared."

"Yeah, me, too," he admitted.

His words echoed back to him. Joanna had been the only one he'd ever let his guard down with, the only one he'd ever allowed to witness his more human, vulnerable side. To the rest of the world, even from a very young age, he'd always presented a strong, unflappable front. It was expected of him. He was a Masters. Only Joanna had seen him as Ricky, as the boy he'd been and the man he was struggling to be.

But all that was behind him. Years behind him.

Rick squared his shoulders. He had to set the tone. What was there to be afraid of, anyway? Taking her hand, he looked down at Joanna. "Babies get born every day, right?"

Yes, but this one was different. This one was coming out of *her*. Shredding everything in its path. "Not this one."

He needed a blanket, a sheet, something. Feeling helpless, Rick looked around. There was nothing available except for the tablecloth he'd used to shield Joanna's face. Taking it, he tucked the material under her as best he could.

"Not exactly sterile, but better than the grass," he explained when she looked at him with huge, questioning eyes.

Oh lord, here came another one. Joanna wrapped her fingers around the long blades of grass, ripping more than a few out of the ground as she arched her back, vainly trying to scramble to a place where the pain couldn't find her.

But there was nowhere to go. The pain found her no matter how she twisted and turned, found her and constructed a wall all around her, imprisoning her.

There was no escape.

Panting again, Joanna tried to recall what she'd learned in her Lamaze classes. Nothing came to her. All she could remember was that the four of them, she, Chris Jones, Sherry Campbell and the instructor, Lori O'Neill, referred to themselves as the Mom

Squad, four single women who'd bonded because they were facing life's most precious miracle alone.

None of that helped now.

She froze, hardly hearing what Rick was saying to her, her body enveloped in one huge contraction.

What was it that Lori'd told the class the last session? Relax, that was it. Relax.

Right, easy for Lori to say. Of the four of them, she was the one who had the longest to go. Lori didn't know what it felt like to be a can of tuna with a jagged can opener circling her perimeter.

But she did.

Joanna let loose with a blood-curling scream as another contraction, the hardest one yet, ripped into her on the tail of the last one. There was no end in sight. She was going to keep on having these contractions until she died.

Rick jerked back, covering his ear. She had risen up and screamed right against it. He could still feel the sound reverberating in his head.

"Good thing I've got two ears. I'm not going to be using my left one for a while."

He shouldn't be the one here, helping her give birth to another man's baby, he thought. This should have been their child fighting its way into the world.

A sadness gripped his heart. He looked at her. "This is all wrong."

With what little strength she had, Joanna dragged her elbows into her sides and struggled to raise herself up again.

"What...? What's...wrong? Something wrong... with...my baby?"

"No, no," he assured her, pushing her gently back

down. "Just that your husband should be here, not me." *Or at least the paramedics,* he added silently.

"Don't...have...one," she gasped. She felt light-headed and fought to keep focused and conscious. Here came another! "Now, Rick, now!"

Rick saw her face turn three shades redder as she screwed her eyes shut.

This was all happening too fast.

He didn't have to tell her to push. He didn't have to tell her anything at all. Suddenly, whether he was ready or not, it was happening. The baby was coming.

Rick barely had enough time to slip his hands into position. The baby's head was emerging. He could feel the blood, feel the slide of flesh against flesh.

Wasn't giving birth supposed to take longer than the amount of time it took to peel a banana skin back?

And why hadn't the fire trucks arrived yet? Were they the last two people on the earth?

It felt that way. The very last two people on earth. Engaged in a life-affirming struggle.

"Pull...it...out!" Joanna screamed. The baby was one-third out, two-thirds in. Why had everything stopped?

She fell back, exhausted, unable to drag in enough air to sustain herself. Beams of light began dancing through her head, motioning her toward them.

Toward oblivion.

In mounting panic, Rick realized that she was going to pass out on him. One hand supporting the baby's head, he leaned over and shook Joanna's shoulder, trying to get her to focus.

"I can't pull it out," he shouted at her. "You can't

play tug of war with a head, Joanna. You have to push the baby out the rest of the way.''

''You...push it out...the...rest of...the way. It's...your...turn.''

And then she felt it again. That horrible pain that she couldn't escape. It bore down on her, tying her up in a knot even as it threatened to crack her apart. It didn't matter that she had no strength, that she couldn't draw a half-decent breath into her lungs. Her body had taken over where her mind had failed.

''Oh...God...it's not...over.'' How was she going to do this with no strength left? How was it possible?

Panting, gasping for air, she looked at Rick. He was right. This was wrong, all wrong. She should never have decided to have this baby, never agreed to leave Rick without explaining why.

Too late now for regrets.

The refrain echoed in her brain over and over again as heat surrounded her, searing a path clear for more pain.

The tablecloth below her was soaked with blood. ''Push,'' Rick ordered gruffly, hiding the mounting fear taking hold of him. What if something went wrong? Should there be this much blood? She couldn't die on him, she couldn't. ''C'mon, Joanna, you can do this!''

No, she thought, she couldn't.

But she had to try. She couldn't just die like this. Her baby needed her.

From somewhere, a last ounce of strength materialized. She bore down as hard as she could, knowing that this was the last effort she was capable of making. If the baby wasn't going to emerge now, they were just going to bury her this way.

Fragments of absurd thoughts kept dancing in and out of her head.

She thought she heard sirens, or screams, in the background. Maybe it was the fire gaining on them. She didn't know, didn't care, she just wanted this all to be over with—one way or another.

She felt as if she was being turned inside out and still she pushed, pushed until her chest felt as if it was caving in, as if her very body was disintegrating from the effort.

And then she heard a tiny cry, softer than all the other noise. Sweeter.

Her head spinning from lack of oxygen, Joanna fell back against the tablecloth, the grass brushing against her soaked neck. She was too exhausted even to breathe.

Rick stared at the miracle in his hands. The miracle was staring back, eyes as wide and huge as her mother's. He felt something twist within him. He was too numb to identify the sensation.

"You've got a girl," he whispered to Joanna, awe stealing his voice away.

He dripped with perspiration, but he knew it was chilly. There was nothing to wrap the baby in. He stripped off his shirt and tucked it around the tiny soul. The infant still watched him with the largest eyes he'd ever seen.

Several feet away from him, a fire truck came to a screeching halt. He hardly acknowledged its arrival. All he could do was look at the baby he'd helped to bring into the world.

Joanna's baby.

The scene around them was almost surreal. People were shouting, firefighters were scrambling down from the truck, running toward them. Running toward the fire.

In the midst of chaos, an older firefighter hurried toward them, his trained eyes assessing the situation quickly. Squatting, he placed a gloved hand on the woman on the ground as well as one on the man holding the newborn. "You two all right?"

"Three," Rick corrected, looking down at the new life tucked against his chest. "And we're doing fine." The smile faded as he looked at Joanna. "I mean—" She'd gone through hell in the last few minutes. He might be fine, but she undoubtedly wasn't. "She needs to get to a hospital."

Rising to his feet, the firefighter nodded. "I can see that." Turning, he signaled to the paramedics, who were just getting out of the ambulance. The firefighter waved them over, then glanced back at Rick as the two hurried over with a gurney. He nodded toward the burning buildings. "Anyone else in there?"

"I don't know." Rick looked to Joanna for confirmation. She shook her head. "I don't think so. I just got here myself," he explained.

"Not just," the firefighter corrected, looking at the baby in Rick's arms.

Rick had no time to make any further comment. A paramedic took the baby from him. He felt a strange loss of warmth as the child left his arms.

"We'll take it from here," the paramedic told him kindly. "Thanks."

The firefighter and a paramedic had already lifted

Joanna onto the gurney. Strapping her in, they raised the gurney and snapped its legs into place.

"You the father?" the first paramedic asked.

Rick was already stepping back. He shook his head in response. "Just a Good Samaritan, in the right place at the right time."

He avoided looking at Joanna when he said it.

She and the baby were already being taken toward the ambulance. The rear doors flew open. Rick remained where he was, watching them being placed inside. For one moment, he had the urge to rush inside, to ride to the hospital with her.

He squelched it.

He was in the way, he thought, stepping back farther as hoses were snaked out and firefighters risked their lives to keep the fire from spreading.

"Lucky for the little lady you were in the neighborhood," the older firefighter commented, raising his voice to be heard above the noise.

The rear lights of the ambulance became brighter as the ignition was engaged. And then it was pulling away from the scene of the fire.

Away from him.

"Yeah, lucky."

Rick turned and walked toward his car. Behind him, the firefighters hurried about the business of trying to stave off the fire before it ate its way down the block and up the hillside.

There was no doubt about it, Rick decided. He should have his head examined.

After he'd gone out to look over the proposed site for the construction of the new corporate home office, instead of returning to the regional office he was temporarily working out of, he'd taken a detour. Actually, it had been two detours.

He'd gone to see just how much damage there'd actually been to Joanna's house. He was hoping, for her sake, that it wasn't as bad as it had looked last night.

In the light of day, the charred remains of the last house on the block—a call to the fire station had informed him that the fire had started there with a faulty electrical timer—looked like a disfigured burned shell. But the firefighters had arrived in time to save at least part of Joanna's house. Only the rear portion was gutted. The front of the house had miraculously sustained a minimum of damage.

Still, he thought, walking around the perimeter, it was going to be a while before the house was livable again.

With a shrug, Rick walked back to his car and got in. Not his problem. That problem belonged to her and her significant other, or whatever she chose to call the man who had fathered her baby.

As far as he was concerned, he'd done as much as he intended to do.

For some reason, after Rick had gone to what was left of Joanna's house, he'd found himself driving toward Blair Memorial Hospital, where the paramedics had taken her last night.

Joanna didn't look surprised to see him walk into her room.

The conversation was awkward, guarded, yet he couldn't get himself to leave.

He had to know.

"You said last night that you weren't married."

He'd promised himself that if he did go to see her, he wasn't going to say anything about her current state. The promise evaporated the moment he saw her.

"I wasn't. I mean, I'm not."

"Divorced?" he guessed.

"No."

"Widowed?"

She sighed, picking at her blanket. Had he turned up in her life just to play Colombo? "No, and I'm not betrothed, either."

She was playing games with him. It shouldn't have bothered him after all this time, but it did. A great deal.

"So, what, this was an immaculate conception?" Sarcasm dripped from his voice. "What's the baby's father's name, Joanna?"

She took a deep breath. "11375."

He stood at the foot of her bed, confusion echoing through his brain. "What?"

"Number 11375." She'd chosen her baby's father from a catalogue offered by the sperm bank. In it were a host of candidates, their identities all carefully concealed. They were known only by their attributes and traits. And a number. "That's all I know him by."

Trying to be discreet, Joanna shifted in her bed. She was still miserably uncomfortable. No one had talked about how sore you felt the day after you gave birth, she thought. Something else she hadn't come across in her prenatal readings.

She raised her eyes to Rick's. His visit had caught her off-guard, but not nearly as much as his appearance in her bedroom last night had. All things considered, it was almost like something out of a movie. A long-ago lover suddenly rushing into her burning bedroom to rescue her. After that, she doubted very much if anything would ever surprise her again.

What kind of double talk was this? "I don't understand. Is he some kind of a spy?"

"No, some kind of a test tube." She saw his brows draw together in a deep scowl. He probably thought she was toying with him. This wasn't exactly something she felt comfortable talking about, but he'd saved her life last night. He deserved to have his question answered. "I went to a sperm bank, Rick."

If ever there was a time for him to be knocked over by a feather, Rick thought, now was it. Maybe he'd just heard her wrong. "Why?"

"Because that's where they keep sperm."

This was an insane conversation. *What are you doing here, Rick? Why are you eight years too late?*

She ran her tongue over her dry lips. "I wanted a baby."

For a second, he couldn't think. Dragging a chair over to her bed, he sank down. "There are other ways to get a baby, Joanna."

Suddenly, she wanted him to go away. This was too painful to discuss. "They all involve getting close to a person."

Memories from the past teased his brain. Memories of moonlit nights, soft, sultry breezes and a woman in his arms he'd vowed to always love. Who'd vowed to always love him.

Always had a short life expectancy.

"They tell me that's the best part," he said quietly.

She looked away. "Been there, done that."

Her flippant tone irritated him. It was on the tip of his tongue to ask if there'd been money involved in this transaction, as well. But the question was too cruel, even if she deserved it. He let it go.

Rick rose, shoving his hand into his pockets as he looked out the window that faced the harbor. "So there's no one else in your life?"

"My baby." Her baby would make her complete, she thought. She didn't need anyone else.

Rick looked at her over his shoulder. "Someone taller."

She knew she should be fabricating lovers, to show him that she could go on with her life, that it hadn't just ended the day they parted, but she was suddenly too tired to make the effort.

"Not in the way you mean, no."

Funny, whenever he'd thought of her in the last eight years, he'd pictured her on someone's arm, laughing the way he loved to see and hear her laugh. It had driven him almost insane with jealousy, but he'd eventually learned how to cope.

Or thought he had until he'd seen her last night, her body filled out with the signs of another man's claim on her.

He turned and looked out on the harbor again. The sky was darkening, even though it was only two in the afternoon. There was a storm coming. Unusual for April. Boats were beginning to leave. "I went by your house this morning."

Her house. Her poor house. Joanna held her breath. "And?"

There was no way to sugarcoat this, but he did his

best. "It was only half destroyed by the fire." Rick turned to look at her. "But it's not habitable." He saw the hopeful light go out of her eyes.

"Damn, now what am I going to do?"

He approached the matter practically. "Well, it's not a total loss. It might take some time to rebuild— you do have coverage, right?"

Yes, she had coverage, but that wasn't why she was upset. Fighting back tears, she sighed. "That's not the point. I was going to take out a home loan on it." The appointment had been postponed from last week. She fervently wished she'd been able to keep it. Now it was too late. "Nobody gives you a loan on the remains of a bonfire." Joanna struggled against the feeling that life had just run her over with a Mack truck. She'd been counting on the money to see her and the baby through the next few months until she could go back to work and start building their future. "Now I don't have the loan or a place to live."

Rick studied her face for a long moment. And then he said the last thing that she expected him to say. The last thing he must have expected himself to say.

"You can come and stay with me."

Three

She stared at Rick, momentarily speechless.

As far as she knew, prenatal vitamins did not fall under the heading of hallucinogenic drugs and she'd had nothing else to throw her brain out of alignment. Why, then was she hearing Rick make an offer she knew he couldn't possibly have made?

"What did you say?"

Her eyes were even bluer than he remembered, bluer and more compelling. He had to struggle not to get lost in them, the way he used to.

"I said, you can come and stay with me—until you get on your feet again," he qualified after a beat, feeling that the offer begged for a coda. This wasn't meant to be a permanent arrangement by any means. He was just temporarily helping a friend. For old times' sake.

If she could have, Joanna would have walked away. As it was, all she could manage was a pugnacious lift of her head.

"I'm sorry, but I don't take charity."

He felt as if she'd insulted him, insulted the memory of what had once been between them. Or had that only been in his own mind? Right at this moment, the chasm that existed between them seemed a hundred yards wide. Sometimes, it was hard to remember how it had gotten this way.

"It would have been charity if I'd just put a wad of bills in your hand and told you not to pay it back." He shrugged, struggling to rein in anger that had materialized out of nowhere. "This is just putting a couple of empty rooms to use."

She assumed by his offer that he was staying at the estate. It was the last place she wanted to be. Not with the past vividly rising up before her. "I really don't think your father would exactly welcome the invasion with open arms."

"One woman and an infant are hardly an invasion—or an intrusion," Rick added before she could revise her words. He guessed at part of the problem. His parents had never treated her with the respect that he'd felt, at the time, that she deserved. His mother was gone now, but there was still his father. "And my father is Florida on vacation." An extended one, he thought. His father hadn't been back to California for several months, actually.

A vacation meant that the man was returning. "So, what's that, a week, two?"

"More like three months or more." With things like teleconferencing, there was not as much need to appear in the flesh anymore, Rick thought. He couldn't say that he disliked the arrangement. The less he saw of his father, the better.

Her mouth curved with a cynicism that was ordinarily foreign to her. "Oh yes, I forgot, the rich are different from you and me—" She glanced up at him. "Well, from me at any rate."

He heard the bitterness in her voice. Was that directed at him? Why? He hadn't said anything to trigger it. But then, as his father had once pointed out, he really didn't know Joanna at all.

Something within him made him push on when another man would have just shrugged and walked away. He wasn't even sure why.

Maybe because, despite the bravado, she looked as if she needed him. Or at least, someone. "Mrs. Rutledge is still there."

At the mention of the woman's name, Joanna's face softened. She and his parents' housekeeper had gotten on very well during the days when he had invited her to his house.

"How is Mrs. Rutledge?"

Like a fighter returning to his corner between rounds, Rick gravitated toward the neutral topic. "Still refusing to retire. Still thinking that she knows what's best for everyone."

Joanna smiled, remembering. "She always reminded me of my mother."

More neutral territory. Rachel Prescott had been the woman he'd secretly wished his mother could have been. He'd spent a great deal of time at Joanna's house over the three years that they went together.

He'd half expected to find her in Joanna's room when he came to visit. "How is your mother?"

"My mother died last year." Joanna looked down at her hands, feeling suddenly hollow. Thirteen months wasn't nearly enough time to grieve.

The news hit him with the force of a bullet. "Oh, I'm sorry." What did a person say at a time like this? How did he begin to express the regret he felt? The world was a sadder place for the loss. He looked at Joanna, his hand covering hers in a mute sympathy be couldn't begin to articulate. "She was a very nice woman."

"Yes, she was." Joanna fought the temptation to stop this awkward waltz they were dancing and throw herself into his arms, to tell him that she'd really needed him those last few months when she had stood by her mother's side, watching the woman who had been her whole world slip away from her. Instead, she looked up at him and said, "I read about your mother in the paper. I'm sorry."

Rick shrugged, letting the perfunctory offer of sympathy pass. It was sad, but he really didn't feel the need for sympathy. He'd never been close to his mother, not even as a child, and consequently, hadn't felt that bitter sting of loss when she died. He'd returned for the funeral like a dutiful son, remaining only long enough for the service to be concluded before flying out again. The entire stay had been less than six hours.

In part, he supposed, he'd left so quickly because he'd wanted to be sure he wouldn't weaken and do exactly what he'd done last night. Drive by Joanna's house. Looking for her.

Joanna tried to fathom the strange expression on his face. She had almost gone to his mother's funeral service at the church, hoping to catch a glimpse of him. But somehow, that had seemed too needy. So instead, she'd shored up her resolve and remained strong, deliberately keeping herself occupied and staying away.

There was another reason she'd kept away. To come to the service would have been to display a measure of respect and she had none for the deceased woman, none for her or her husband. Not since the two had joined forces that August day and come to her bearing a sizable check with her name on it.

All she had to do to earn it was to get out of their son's life, they'd said. To sweeten the pot, they'd appealed to her sense of fair play, to her love for Rick. Between the two of them, they'd projected the future and what it would be like for Rick if he married her. They were adamant that he would grow to despise her. He belonged, they maintained, with his own kind. With a woman from his social world, with his background and his tastes. Someone who could be an asset to him, not a liability. They'd even had someone picked out. A woman she knew by sight.

They argued so well that she'd finally had to agree. She hated them for that, for making her see how much better off Rick would be without her.

"Actually," Rick commented on her original protest, "if there is any charity being dispensed, you'd be the one doing it."

He always was good with words, she thought. But he had lost her this time. "Come again? I think I pushed out my hearing along with the baby."

The laugh was soft. He began to feel a little more comfortable. Despite the hurt feelings that existed between them like a third, viable entity, Joanna had always had the knack of being able to make him relax.

"If Mrs. Rutledge finds out that you're homeless," he explained, "and that I knew about it, she'll have me filleted."

"I'm not homeless," she protested. "Just temporarily unhoused."

It was an offer, she supposed in all honesty, that she couldn't refuse. She knew she could probably crash on any one of a number of sofas, but she would also be bringing her baby and that was an imposition she wasn't willing to make. Babies made noise, they took getting used to. It was an unfair strain to place on any friendship. Rick had the only house where the cries of a child wouldn't echo throughout the entire dwelling. Where she wouldn't be in the way as she struggled to find her footing in this new world of motherhood.

Joanna chewed on her lip, vacillating. "You're sure your father's away?"

For a moment, Rick was transported back through time, sitting in math class, watching her puzzle out an equation. He smiled, fervently wishing he could somehow go back and relive that period of his life.

But all he had available to him was the present.

"I spoke to him this morning via conference hook-up. He's having a great time marlin-fishing off the Florida Keys."

Joanna tried to picture the stuffy man sitting at the stern of a boat, a rod and reel clutched in his hands, and failed. "Marlin-fishing? Your father?"

He knew it sounded far-fetched, but it was true. Howard Masters had undergone nothing short of a transformation. "The heart attack turned him into a new man. He might not be stopping to smell the roses, but he is taking time to do almost everything else."

The man had always been consumed with making money. She'd heard that he'd only taken one day off when his wife died. "What about the business?"

"Mostly, it's in my hands." He wondered if that made her think that he'd become his father. The thought brought a shiver down his spine. "He likes to look over my shoulder every so often and make 'suggestions.' But mostly, he leaves it all up to me."

She wondered if Rick would eventually turn into his father. There was a time when she would have said no, but that was about a man she'd loved. A man who had failed to live up to her expectations. "Is that why you're here?"

Eyebrows drew together over an almost perfect nose. "In the hospital?"

"No, in Bedford. Did the family business bring you to Bedford?" He nodded. She knew she should leave it at that, but she couldn't help asking, "And why were you outside my house last night?"

He gave her the most honest answer he could, given the situation. "I'm not really sure."

Fair enough. Joanna blew out a breath, shifting slightly again, trying not to pay attention to the discomfort radiating from her lower half. *This too, shall pass.*

"Well, I can't say I'm not glad you were." She

raised her eyes to his. "Otherwise—" her voice, filled with emotion, trailed off.

He stopped her before she could continue. "I've learned that 'otherwise' is not a street that takes travel well." There was nothing to be gained by second-guessing. "You get too bogged down going there."

He heard the door just behind him being opened. Welcoming the respite, Rick turned and saw a nurse wheeling in a clear bassinet. Inside, bundled in a pink blanket, sleeping peacefully, was possibly the most beautiful baby he'd ever seen.

"Someone's going to be waking up soon and it's feeding time," the woman announced. Her smile took in both of them.

Rick moved out of the way as the nurse brought the bassinet closer, his eyes riveted to the small occupant. "Wow."

The single word filled her with pride. Joanna couldn't help smiling. "I believe that's her first compliment."

"But not her last," Rick guaranteed. "She cleans up nicely."

"You got to see her at her worst," Joanna pointed out. She didn't add that he'd seen her at possibly her worst as well.

Rick sincerely doubted that the word *worst* could be applied to a miracle. Something stirred within him as he watched the nurse lift the infant from the bassinet and hand her over to Joanna.

He was in the way, he thought. "Well, I'd better be going." He began to edge his way out.

Suddenly, she didn't want him to leave. Not yet. "Would you like to hold her?" Joanna asked.

Somehow, the baby looked far more fragile now than she had last night. And his hands were large and clumsy. "I already did."

"I mean now that she's not messy." Joanna read his expression correctly. "She won't break, you know. Not if you're gentle."

"I won't slam dunk her," he promised. The quip was meant to hide what was really going on inside him. There were emotions there that he wasn't sure he understood or knew what to do with. Certainly none that he could label properly.

Very carefully, he slipped his hands under the baby's back and neck, making the transfer. He unintentionally brushed his fingers against Joanna's breasts. Their eyes met and held for a moment before he backed away from her, holding the infant to him.

The nurse looked on and nodded with approval. "You're a natural."

"He should be," Joanna told her. "He's the one who held her first."

The woman's smile brightened. "Oh, are you her father?"

"No." The nurse's innocent question dragged him away from the formless region he'd momentarily found himself inhabiting and back to the real world. He wasn't the little girl's father and that was the whole point. "I'm not." He handed the infant back to Joanna. "I'll be back before you're discharged."

There was a formal note in his voice that she didn't understand or like. The temporary bridge between their two worlds was gone and they were back to being wounded strangers again.

"We'll see," she called after him. She had the satisfaction of seeing him momentarily halt before continuing out the door.

Like a commando unit making a beachhead, the three other women who comprised the Mom Squad descended upon Joanna as one later that afternoon, brightening her spirit as well as her room.

They came bearing gifts, and, more importantly, they came bearing good will and cheer. Something she was finding temporarily in short supply.

The baby was awake and alert and seemed very willing to be passed from one woman to the other like a precious doll.

Sherry Campbell, newly returned to the working world as a reporter for the *Bedford World News* and a brand-new mother in her own right, was the first to hold her. The baby was almost as big as Sherry's own three-month-old son. But then, Johnny had been a preemie.

"She's beautiful." She beamed at Joanna. "Of course, that's not a surprise. Look at her mother."

Chris Jones, a special agent with the FBI, coaxed the baby out of her friend's arms. She tucked the newborn against her, partially resting the infant against her own rounded stomach. "Too bad we don't know what the father looks like."

Lori O'Neill laughed. "Well, he was obviously not a frog."

Sherry frowned thoughtfully as she looked at the others. Joanna's method of becoming pregnant was a matter of record. "Do sperm banks allow ugly men to contribute their um, genes?"

"Apparently not," Chris cracked. She handed the infant over to Lori and then moved around to the side of Joanna's bed. She perched on a corner, though it wasn't easy. "So tell me, was it awful?"

"Was what awful?" Joanna asked.

Chris hesitated. "Giving birth. Was it like getting shot?"

Joanna pressed her lips together, trying not to laugh at the question. She knew that Chris was nervous about this unknown territory they all had to face on their own. "I've never been shot, so my field of reference is a little limited."

Chris backtracked. "Okay, was it like what you imagine getting shot is like?"

Lori rolled her eyes. She'd never given birth herself, but she'd talked to scores of mothers. The comparison was unusual, to say the least. "Chris—"

"Well, I've been shot," Chris insisted, "and that was the worst pain I've ever physically had, but it was okay." She looked at the others, feeling herself grow defensive. "I'm just trying to put things into perspective here."

Sherry pretended to shake her head as she leaned in to "confide" to Joanna. "You'd think that a woman who was with the FBI, who'd gone through some pretty scary situations and lived to tell about it wouldn't be so afraid of giving birth."

Chris tossed her long blond hair over her shoulder. "I'm not afraid of giving birth, I just want to be prepared, that's all. The first thing you learn as an agent is never to walk into a room you don't know how to get out of—"

"The only way to 'get out of' this particular 'room'

at this point is to give birth," Lori told her, "so you'd just better resign yourself to that. Relax," she gave Chris's shoulder a playful pat, "it's not as bad as you think."

"Why didn't you ask Sherry?" Joanna asked. After all, the vivacious reporter had been the first of them to go through childbirth, and if anyone could fill Chris in on the darker side of giving birth, it was Sherry. She'd delivered her baby in a desolate mountain cabin with only a dog and a reclusive billionaire in attendance. Lucky for her, the man had been a jack of all trades, up to and including being a one-time pre-med student.

Chris sighed, picking at the design on the blanket. "Because all Sherry'll tell me is the official party line." Chris rolled her eyes and parroted the famous edict uttered by mothers since the beginning of time: "You forget all about the pain as soon as you hold the baby in your arms."

"Well, you do," Joanna insisted. And she had already—for the most part. "Except when you try to shift your bottom."

Sherry and Lori laughed, but Chris looked at her seriously. "So it's awful?"

"Awful?" Joanna repeated, examining the word. "No, not really. It's not exactly something I'd recommend doing for pleasure," her eyes slid over toward the baby, who was back in Sherry's arms, "but it is definitely worth it. Trust me."

The baby began to fuss a little. Sherry patted the tiny bottom and the fussing stopped. "So, I hear you didn't make it to the hospital, either."

Joanna laughed shortly. "I almost didn't make it

anywhere. My house was on fire when I went into labor.''

Lori's eyes widened. "Oh my God, we didn't know. How's your house?''

Joanna remembered how terrified she'd been as they put her into the back of the ambulance. The last thing she saw as they closed the doors was the wall of flames closing in around her house.

"Still standing, they tell me. The fire chief came by to see me earlier today and said they managed to save part of it, but right now, it's not habitable.''

There but for the grace of God, Sherry thought. She knew all about Joanna's situation and her financial predicament. Like Joanna, she'd been eased out of her job. Hers had been a high-profile position as lead anchor woman for the local news station. If it hadn't been for some string-pulling that had landed her on the newspaper, she would have been in the same place as Joanna now. Unemployed. The only difference being she had her family to lean on. Joanna didn't.

Sherry leaned over and squeezed Joanna's hand. "You can come and stay with me.'' Sherry grinned. "We can start a baby co-op.''

But Joanna shook her head. "You have a new baby and a new man in your life, the last thing you need right now is another woman with a newborn.''

Lori was quick to interrupt. "You can crash at my place.''

Joanna laughed. She knew Lori meant well, but it wasn't possible. "I've seen your place. It's a broom closet. Not even *you* can really crash there.''

Lori knew she had a point. She'd been looking at

apartment rentals ever since she'd found out she was pregnant. "I'm looking for a new place."

"Well, there's always me," Chris offered. "My place is bigger than a bread box," she pointed out.

Joanna had already made up her mind, however. "Thank you, all of you, really, but I have a place to stay."

Sherry second-guessed her. There were times that Joanna had just too much pride. "You can't stay at a hotel. They charge exorbitant rates and—"

Joanna cut her off. "It's not a hotel. It's the Masters estate."

The other three exchanged looks. Chris was the first to recover. "What? How did this happen?"

Joanna decided to go with the abridged version. No one knew about her and Rick and, for the time being, she wanted to keep it that way. Maybe for all time, she thought. "It happened when Rick Masters rescued me from my burning bedroom."

Lori recalled seeing something in the newspaper. "Didn't I just read that he was spending time in Florida?"

Joanna nearly choked. She could just see Howard Masters rushing in to save her. "Not the father, the son."

A slow, appreciative smile curved Sherry's lips. She'd seen photographs of Richard Masters. Definitely not a face that stopped a clock. A heart, maybe, but not a clock. "Oh, the son."

Chris was familiar with the man. "Wow, talk about a fairy-tale meeting—"

"It wasn't our first." The words had popped out before she could stop them.

Lori made herself comfortable on the bed. "Have you been holding out on us?"

"Just someone from my past." Joanna shrugged dismissively.

"Details, we want details," Chris begged. She exchanged glances with Lori. "You know how hungry for romance pregnant women get."

Joanna searched for a tactful way out. "It all happened a long time ago."

"Doesn't matter," Sherry urged her on, "tell us."

Oh, what the hell did it matter? After all, these were her friends, women who had already shown, more than once, that they cared about her. "We were supposed to get married."

"And?" all three cried almost in unison.

She sighed. The memory still bothered her, even after all this time. "And his parents convinced me that I was all wrong for him. That Loretta Langley was the woman he should build his future with."

"Hate the woman already," Lori told her. "Who was she?"

"Someone from his side of the tracks."

"Tracks don't matter unless you're a train," Chris told her firmly. "I hope you told those people where to go."

Maybe she should have, but her mother hadn't raised her that way. And besides, Rick's parents had been very, very persuasive and thorough. "No, like I said, they convinced me."

"But not him," Chris told her.

The matter-of-fact tone had her pausing. "What do you mean?"

"Well, you do the math. He just 'happened' to be

there to rescue you, right?'' It didn't take a profiler to see through this case. ''Unless the man's a demented pyromaniac who sets up his own heroic scenarios, I'd say he still had a thing for you.''

Joanna waved away the conclusion. She wasn't about to set herself up for another fall, not after all this time. ''I doubt it.''

But Sherry backed Chris up. ''He offered to let you stay with him, didn't he?''

''He could offer to let the population of Scotland stay with him and not really notice. It's a very big house,'' Joanna insisted when she saw the others exchange looks.

Her own husband's house had been virtually empty before she'd come into his life, Sherry thought. Size had nothing to do with it. It was who was there to fill it that mattered. ''I'd say the lady doth protest too much, wouldn't you?'' She looked at the others, who nodded.

Sherry's comment fell on deaf ears as far as Joanna was concerned. They could say whatever they wanted. It still didn't change what was. For whatever reason he'd shown up in her life now, Rick had gotten over her a long time ago. To believe anything else would just be deluding herself and right now, she thought as she looked at her baby, she had more important things to think about.

Four

Never mind that he'd already made two appearances in her life in the last two days, the first of which would always rank as spectacular, each time Joanna saw Rick walking toward her, it didn't fail to surprise her, at least to some degree.

This time, he actually came with a surprise of his own as well. Nodding a greeting at her, Rick deposited a large rectangular box on top of her blanket-covered legs.

Despite the fact that the logo on the box proclaimed it to be from a department store that catered predominantly to a clientele whose incomes began in the six-figure range, Joanna stared at it blankly. There was no wrapping paper, no card to declare its purpose, not even a ribbon to proclaim a feeble attempt at festivity. He just placed it before her and then took a step back, like someone admiring his own handiwork.

Not touching the box, she raised her eyes to his. "What's this?"

Rick curbed his impatience, telling himself that what was inside was utilitarian and not a gift. But a sense of anticipation refused to abate. He wanted to see the expression on her face when she opened it. "It's a box."

"I can see that." She fingered it tentatively. Was he giving her a gift? Was he trying to say he was sorry for not coming after her eight years ago? No, that was stupid. She was sure he probably didn't think about that at all. Not the way she did. "What's in it?"

He almost leaned over and opened the box for her, but at the last minute, he shoved his hands into his pockets. "Only one way to find out that I know of—unless you've acquired X-ray vision along with that suspicious mind of yours."

She raised her chin, a hint of defensiveness evident in the motion. "I am not suspicious."

Rick laughed shortly. From where he stood, it felt as if she was questioning all his motives. "Then what would you call it?"

"Being cautious." Joanna shrugged carelessly. The sleeve of her hospital gown went sliding off her shoulder and she pushed it back up. "Once burned, twice leery, that kind of thing."

He didn't want to go where she was leading. There was no point in going over that ground. "You were burned by a box?"

Joanna pressed her lips together. He knew damn well what she was saying. "No, by a feeling."

He looked at her. What was she implying? He'd

been the one to get hurt back then, not her. She'd made a tidy profit out of it as well. "Well, maybe that makes two of us."

Exasperated, he gave up waiting. Rick reached over and lifted the top of the box for her, shaking it slightly so that it would come loose. The bottom rose with it, then separated. As the box fell, its contents came tumbling out, revealing a two-piece red suit.

He remembered, she thought, stunned. There'd been a red suit she'd once pointed out to him, saying that she loved the way that it looked. This suit was almost identical to that one.

But that was eight years ago. It had to be a coincidence.

And yet…

"Clothes?" She tried to read his expression. There was no indication that he knew what the red suit meant. "You bought me clothes?"

He picked up the pale cream blouse that had been packed under the suit and had slid off the bed when the box opened. He placed it next to the outfit. Rick nodded at what she was wearing.

"Well, you're being sprung soon and I didn't think the hospital was going to let you keep that fetching gown they issued you. I happen to know for a fact that there are laws on the books against parading around in public without any clothes—even with a body like yours."

She ran her fingers over the fabric. She knew the kind of price tags that went with outfits like this. There was no way she could have afforded to buy it for herself. But somehow, she was going to find the money to pay him back. She was her own person and not to be bought, even by acts of kindness.

Joanna laughed shortly at his comment. "Thanks for the compliment, but it's been a while since you've seen this body."

She knew, to the day, just how long it had been since they'd been together as lovers. How many years, how many months, how many days. No matter how many other things she filled her head with, that information somehow always managed to remain.

He wondered if she even remembered pointing out that red suit to him. Probably not. He was being too sentimental. Funny, he would have thought that there was no sentiment left in him. All it took to bring it out was being with her.

Rick shrugged. "There was that encounter a couple of days ago," he quipped.

Color shot up to her cheeks. "You know what I mean."

"Yes, I do and yes it has been a long time since I admired your body in the very best sense of the word." His eyes swept over her. "But I'd still be willing to bet that you look better than ninety-eight percent of the female population."

Her eyes filled with amusement. "Ninety-eight percent, huh? My, you have been busy. When did you get any time to pay attention to business?"

"Slight exaggeration," he allowed, sitting down in the chair beside her bed. "The kind, if I recall correctly, that you used to be given to." It was a throwaway line. He recalled everything there was to remember about her. That was his curse, the reason he could never get himself to settle down and start a family the way his friends all had. The way his parents kept insisting that he do. He nodded toward the box. "That should fit you."

She glanced inside the jacket. It was the right size. "You've got a good eye."

"More like a good memory. I did buy you that sweater one Christmas."

A sadness waft through her. The sweater had been retired to a keepsake box, along with every single word he'd ever written to her and every photograph of the two of them she'd had. The box had been in her closet. It was undoubtedly a casualty of the fire. It was as if she wasn't even allowed to hang onto her memories.

She tried to keep the tears back.

"What's the matter?"

"Nothing," she sniffed. "Allergies."

He scrutinized her face. She was lying. "I don't remember you having allergies."

Joanna waved her hand vaguely. "It comes and goes." Very carefully, she placed the jacket back into the box on top of the skirt. She folded the blouse, leaving it on top of both, then closed the lid over them. "Thank you."

He took the box from her, placing it on the shelf against the wall. "You're welcome."

He was still thoughtful. It was nice to know that some things hadn't changed. "I hadn't thought about what I was going to wear," she confessed. Her daughter, on the other hand, was all taken care of. All she had to do was choose an outfit from the gifts that Lori, Sherry and Chris had brought her.

He had a feeling clothes had slipped her mind.

When he'd gone back to her house a second time to closely assess the damage, he'd also taken inventory of her clothes. Nothing had been spared. It was just sheer luck that he'd found her purse on the living-room coffee table. Aside from the smoke damage, it was still intact.

"You were never detail-oriented."

"No," she agreed, "that was always your department." That was what had made them so perfect together, they complemented one another. Whatever trait one lacked, the other possessed. It was as if they were meant to be one whole person. Or so she'd tried to tell herself at the time.

Had she ever really been that innocent? To actually believe in soul mates?

For a moment, Rick sat there in silence, looking at her and wondering what had happened to them. Why had things gone so wrong? They'd had so much going for them.

And then he laughed to himself. He knew the answer to that. In part, he blamed his family for what had happened, but he couldn't help blaming her as well. All she'd had to do was love him, to have faith in him and know that he would have made everything right.

But she'd allowed herself to be lied to. To be bought off. That had been the real end of any dreams that might have been. She'd allowed money to come between them. Just as his parents had predicted.

The touch of her hand on his had him pulling out of the daze his thoughts had taken him into. She was staring at him. "What?"

He had such a strange expression on his face. As if he were a million miles away. "Where are you?"

"Right here," he said shortly, embarrassed at being caught. "I was just thinking, that's all."

And she had a feeling she knew about what. "Having second thoughts about the arrangement?"

"No." The denial was sharp. He forced a smile to his lips, or what might have passed for one, had she not known what he was capable of. "Just thinking," he repeated.

He was shutting her out. Well, what did she expect? That they would suddenly pick up where they'd left off eight years ago? Did she expect him to sweep her off her feet, tell her that nothing else mattered except that he loved her and would always love her?

She wasn't twenty anymore, wasn't naive anymore. There was no such thing as happily ever after, not for her and Rick at any rate.

Still, she heard herself pressing, wanting him to be truthful with her. "About what?"

About how something wonderful could have turned out so badly. He rose to his feet. "What time are they signing you out tomorrow?"

Mentally, she retreated to her corner. His kindness had thrown her off for a minute, but she was okay now. Able to handle things as they came. "Before noon. My insurance won't cover another day."

He frowned. Something didn't sound right. "I thought the teachers' union had a good insurance plan?"

"They do." And she wished she could still have it. But the COBRA payments that would have allowed her to carry on her insurance after termination had been far too expensive for her even to consider. "Mine's an individual policy." She took a breath before telling him. "I'm not a teacher anymore."

He stared at her. When they'd been together, all she could talk about was becoming a teacher. It had been her goal ever since she'd been six years old. And one of the things his mother had found abhorrent. "You loved being a teacher."

"I still do." She struggled to keep the note of bitterness out of her voice. Like everything else, this was just a hurdle she had to get over. "But the one thing I failed to factor in when I made my decision to become a single mother was that the local school board would be uncomfortable with my single state coupled with my distended body. Simply put, they didn't feel that I was setting a good example for the children. So, they asked me to 'go on an extended leave of absence.'"

"No money," he guessed.

"No money."

She was as feisty as he remembered. Another woman would have crumbled in her situation. "So you're unemployed."

Joanna preferred to put her own spin on it. Raising her chin, she told him, "I am temporarily between positions."

He laughed, shaking his head. "Damn, but you are unsinkable, aren't you?"

"I try to be. Things have a way of working themselves out." She looked at him pointedly. "Who would ever have thought you'd come charging through the flames to rescue me?"

"Who would have thought," he echoed. Taking

out a PalmPilot, he pulled up his schedule and made a notation with his stylus. "I'll be here before eleven," he promised, then tucked the PalmPilot into the pocket of his jacket. He saw her smiling and shaking her head. "What?"

"I just had a flashback." She grinned. "Remember how you used to say that you were never going to be anything like your father?"

Momentarily stepping into the past, he couldn't help recalling other things he'd said to her. Like pledging his undying love. It sounded hokey now, but he'd meant it then with a fierceness that had taken even him by surprise.

Life had a way of changing things.

Rick brushed his fingers along the outline of her cheek. "I used to say a lot of things." And so had she. He dropped his hand to his side. There was no point in going there. He'd learned his lesson. Words were usually empty, forgotten moments after they were uttered. "Times change."

She raised her eyes to his. *Maybe I was wrong to believe your parents, maybe I was wrong to leave you, but you were wrong, too. You didn't come after me, didn't try to make me change my mind.* "Yes, they do, but people don't have to."

He deliberately turned his thoughts to the business world. "They do if they want to grow. If you don't move forward, you slide backwards."

That was his father talking, not him. Had he become his father these last years? She didn't want to believe it, didn't want to think of him that way. "Not necessarily. There's nothing wrong with standing still."

There is if you're trying to stay one step ahead of memories that can undo you. He looked at her for a long moment. "I'll see you tomorrow." With that, he turned away and began to walk out.

She felt a pang squeeze her heart. What was she doing, trying to torture herself? She still had some money saved. "Rick."

His hand on the door, he stopped and looked over his shoulder. "What?"

"I can still go to a hotel."

"Mrs. Rutledge is expecting you. I'll see you tomorrow."

And with that, he left.

She glanced over to her sleeping daughter, and fervently prayed that men found a way to evolve in the next fifteen years, before her baby got involved in her own whirlwind.

"Sometimes, Rach, men are more trouble than they are worth."

But even as she said it, Joanna knew she didn't really believe it.

It felt as if every cloud in Southern California had converged above Bedford the next day. The storm began at around six in the morning and promised to continue until the evening without any letup.

"If it'd rained like this three days ago, my house would still be standing," Joanna commented as she took the seat beside Rick in the Mercedes.

Behind her, Rachel lay strapped into a baby seat. Joanna had been surprised to see that he had thought to get one for the baby. The tab on the items she owed him for was growing.

If it had rained like this three nights ago, he would have just kept going after passing her house. There would have been no need to rescue her, no need to deliver her baby. And no need to bring her into his life, however temporarily.

Fate was a very strange thing. It both took and gave.

He glanced toward her. She was quiet. He couldn't remember her ever being quiet. "Tired?"

"A little." And more than slightly apprehensive that she was making another wrong decision.

"We'll be there soon," he promised.

"I remember the way."

She remembered far more than that, she thought, and that was part of the problem. How insane was it, to walk back into the past like this?

But it wasn't the past, not really. She was a mother now, and he had moved on with his life, too. They were just two people who'd once shared a past, nothing more.

Despite the storm and the frantic rhythm of the windshield wipers, Joanna could make out the form of a tall, thin woman standing at the entrance of the house, a huge umbrella in her hand, poised to go into action at a moment's notice.

The instant she saw them, Mrs. Rutledge opened the umbrella and hurried toward the passenger side of the car, prepared to protect and serve to the best of her ability. Some things, Joanna thought with a surge of warmth, *didn't* change.

"There's Mrs. Rutledge," Joanna heard herself saying. "Won't she catch cold?"

He wondered if Joanna was aware that she sounded excited. "No germ would dare try to incapacitate Mrs. Rutledge. I've never known her to be sick a day in her life. Or at least, not a day in mine."

The next thing Joanna knew, her door was being opened. The scent of vanilla dueled with the smell of the rain and won.

"My dear, how pale you look." The woman's light-green eyes shifted accusingly toward Rick before becoming compassionate again as she looked at Joanna.

"Hello, Mrs. Rutledge." Joanna smiled warmly at her. There was no evidence of any change in the housekeeper. She still had iron-gray hair, worn short, still dressed in a light-gray shirt-front uniform that came mid-way down her calves. "How are you?"

"Ready to bring a little color back into your cheeks, you can count on that."

After over fifty years, there was still just the barest hint of a Southern drawl in her voice. Nadine Smith Rutledge hailed from South Carolina, the seventh of fifteen children born to a coal miner and his wife. They'd all gone on to earn their own way in the world as soon as they were old enough to work. Only Nadine had made it out this far west. She'd come to work for Rick's grandfather and stayed on through the generations, making herself indispensable along the way.

The housekeeper peered into the back seat, her face softening considerably. "And this must be your little one. One forgets how tiny they start out." She looked over at Rick. She took on the tone more suitable for a headmistress than a housekeeper. "Well, don't just sit there, come around to my side and hold the umbrella while I help Miss Joanna and her baby out."

"Yes'm." Tolerant amusement surrounded the single word. Rick hurried out of the car, rounding the hood. He took the umbrella from the older woman, holding it aloft as Joanna got out. It was large enough to provide shelter for all three of them.

Mrs. Rutledge carefully unfastened the straps around the infant. Cornflower-blue eyes opened wide to watch her. "She's got your eyes, Miss Joanna. And your fair skin." With gentle hands she drew the baby out of her seat. "Going to be a beauty, she is, mark my words. Oh my," she murmured as she brought the bundle of softness to her chest. "I haven't held a little one in my arms since I took care of Mr. Rick here." Mrs. Rutledge glanced over her shoulder at him. "Hard to believe he was ever this small, isn't it?"

Rick cleared his throat. "Could we get Joanna and her baby out of the rain before we go traveling down memory lane, Mrs. Rutledge?"

"Hope your baby's got a better disposition than that one," she commented to Joanna.

With her arms wrapped firmly around her small charge and Rick holding the umbrella over her head, Mrs. Rutledge led the way to the front door. Joanna pressed her lips together, trying not to smile. The woman made her think of Queen Victoria strolling about Windsor Castle.

Castle was the word for it, Joanna thought a moment later.

Or maybe *mausoleum* was a better one. She'd always felt that the house where Rick had grown up had all the warmth of a stone. Nothing seemed to have changed. If anything, it felt even colder.

"I know, I know," Mrs. Rutledge commented, glancing at her face. "It has all the hominess of a cave, but now that Mr. Rick is here, I suspect there'll be some changes made. Won't there?" She peered at him pointedly as he shut the front door.

After closing the umbrella, Rick deposited it in a large metal umbrella stand his mother had bought on one of her frequent shopping trips to Paris. It was shaped like an African elephant. Water cascaded along the elephant's face, making it appear as if it was crying.

He felt absolutely no attachment to this place. "I'm here to set up a new corporate home office, Mrs. Rutledge," he reminded her, "not to redecorate the house."

"Still, if you're moving back here, you're going to need to make some changes. Make this more of a home." Her eyes sparkled as she turned them toward Joanna. "I've been making up this list of renovations for the last few years."

Joanna looked at Rick. He'd told her his father was away on vacation. "Doesn't Mr. Masters still live here?"

Mrs. Rutledge dismissed the obstacle with a wave of her hand. "He's hardly been here in the last six months. He's become a changed man since his heart attack."

"So I've been told."

"Enough about that, you two need to rest. Let me show you where you'll be staying," Mrs. Rutledge said. Turning on her heel, she led Joanna to a room located on the first floor in the east wing of the house.

Since Mrs. Rutledge had taken over, this was his cue to leave, Rick thought. But he decided he could spare a few more minutes. Besides, he wanted to see the expression on Joanna's face when she saw the nursery.

Moving around them, Rick opened the door to the first room and then allowed Joanna to go in ahead of him. "It's yours for as long as you want."

Done in pale blues and whites, it looked like a bedroom out of a dream. He'd remembered that blue was her favorite color, she thought, or was that its original color and she was just reading too much into it?

"The nursery's right through here." Mrs. Rutledge opened the door to a small adjoining room. "This gets the morning sun," she told her. Right now, rain pounded against the panes. "When it's available."

Joanna crossed to the crib, looking at it in awe. It was an antique. Mrs. Rutledge placed the baby in it, then covered the infant with a blanket.

Joanna looked at the woman. "Where did you—?"

"This used to be Mr. Rick's. I had it taken out of storage when I heard you would be staying with us."

"Temporarily," Joanna interjected.

"We're all here temporarily, Miss Joanna," Mrs. Rutledge replied. "On our way to other places." She smiled warmly. "No reason we can't be comfortable while we're here, is there?"

Joanna slanted a glance toward Rick. Damn, but her heart was going to be in jeopardy again, she just knew it. "That depends on what that comfort costs."

"Not a dime, Joanna, not a dime."

She turned to him. "You know I can't accept all this."

"We'll discuss it later," he told her. "I've got to be going." She still looked frail to him somehow. Squelching the protective feeling stirring within him, he drew Joanna aside. "You'll be all right?"

"I have Mrs. Rutledge, how could I not be?" She looked around her. "You really didn't have to go to all this trouble, you know."

Maybe not, but he'd wanted to. Maybe she still had some kind of hold on him, despite everything. "I didn't," he lied. "All I did was tell Mrs. Rutledge and she did the rest." He caught Mrs. Rutledge looking at him. The woman, he knew, didn't approve of lies.

He was lying, Joanna thought. She could always tell when he was lying. His tone changed. Moved, she brushed a kiss against his check. He jerked back as if she'd burned him.

Flustered, she took a step back herself. "Sorry."

"Don't be." Stupid to overreact that way, he upbraided himself. It was just that he didn't want to start anything. *Then why did you bring her here?* "It's just been a while, that's all."

Despite his resolve, Rick couldn't hold back the warmth that insisted on spreading through him. There'd been women since Joanna had left his life. A host of women. In the beginning, he'd tried to lose himself in them, to engage in hot, mindless sex intended to burn away her very memory. It didn't, and he'd learned soon enough how futile that effort was.

Even so, for a year after he'd left Bedford, he'd

forced himself to remain active on the social scene until he'd finally abandoned the futile effort.

No one had ever affected him the way she had.

You never forget your first love. Mrs. Rutledge had told him that. Mrs. Rutledge had an annoying habit of being right.

"I leave her in your capable hands, Mrs. Rutledge," he said to the housekeeper. With that, he left the room.

"He's never been the same, you know," the woman confided once Rick was safely out the door. "Not since you left." Mrs. Rutledge silently closed the nursery door and gently ushered Joanna to her bed. "I just thought you'd want to know that."

Joanna didn't want to talk about this, didn't want to feel guilty about doing something that had cost her more than anyone could ever guess. "Mrs. Rutledge—"

The woman held up her hands. "I'm not asking you why you broke it off with him. I'm sure you had your reasons. It's none of my affair what happened between the two of you." She drew back the comforter and waited for Joanna to sit down. "I just think you should know that you were the only ray of sunshine this house had seen in a very long time and when you left, the light went out. Out of the house and out of his eyes."

She spread the comforter over Joanna much the way she had over the baby, then crossed to the doorway. "I'll just be down the hall. Call me if there's anything you need. *Anything,*" she underlined.

Suddenly exhausted, Joanna was having trouble

keeping her eyes open. ''I just want to close my eyes for a few minutes.''

The woman nodded her approval as she slowly eased the door closed.

Five

The sound of persistent tapping made its way into Joanna's consciousness, rousing her brain and lifting it from the depths of sleep. Raindrops, she realized. Raindrops were hitting the window panes.

Joanna forced her eyes open. The room was nestled in darkness.

She wasn't alone.

She bolted upright, a sense of fear blanketing her. The shape she'd vaguely discerned took on form. Rick was standing beside the bed, looking down at her.

"Wha-what are you doing here?"

He grinned, the left corner of his mouth rising a little higher than the right. She'd teased him more than once about his lop-sided grin.

"You keep asking me that. My house, remember?"

It took a second, but she did remember. Remember everything. The fire, Rachel being born, Mrs. Rutledge. She sighed. "Oh, right. I remember."

"You feel up to dinner? Or do you want me to have Mrs. Rutledge bring you a tray?"

She couldn't allow herself to be waited on, no matter how tempting. "I'm not an invalid."

"I'll take that as a no." Rick crossed to the doorway. "Mrs. Rutledge is right outside. I'll see you in the dining room," he told her as he left.

She felt foolish. She'd only meant to close her eyes for a few minutes. How long had she been asleep? She glanced at the clock on the night stand.

"Omigod," she cried out loud, "it's almost six o'clock. I slept over five hours."

Mrs. Rutledge stuck her head in from the nursery. "Certainly looks that way."

When Rick had said the housekeeper was outside, she'd thought he meant the hallway. She didn't realize he was talking about the nursery. Joanna quickly swung her legs down from the bed. "The baby—"

For an older woman, Mrs. Rutledge knew how to move fast without giving the impression of moving at all. She was beside her before Joanna could finish her sentence, placing a hand on her shoulder to keep the new mother from leaping up and possibly hurting something.

"She's fine, dear. I've been in to check on her several times." She smiled warmly at Joanna. "You, too. You were easier. You didn't need any changing or feeding."

It was her responsibility to care for the baby, not the housekeeper's. Some mother she made. Joanna dragged her hand through her hair and looked at the other woman, guilt nibbling away at her. "You changed her?"

Because it was already dark, Mrs. Rutledge went to the windows and began drawing the drapes.

"I'm from a large family, dear. Took care of my share of babies. Things haven't changed all that much. One end eats, the other eliminates." She saw Joanna looking toward the next room. "You can reassure yourself about Rachel's condition and even have enough time to freshen up before dinner."

"Dinner," Joanna echoed, trying to straighten out the jumble in her head. "Rick said something about that just now."

She wasn't altogether sure she was up to facing him over a meal. She'd had some pretty erotic dreams just now, all of which had involved him. With their effect still hovering over her brain, it became rather difficult for her to remember to keep her distance from him.

Mrs. Rutledge crossed back to her, folding her hands rather primly before her.

"He arrived home half an hour ago." She smiled. "He came in and checked on you himself, couldn't believe you were still sleeping. He also took over Rachel's last feeding."

She stared at the housekeeper as if the woman had just told her Rick had sprouted wings and flown over the house. "He fed Rachel?"

The woman nodded. "Didn't do that bad a job of it, either." Mrs. Rutledge smiled. "Man's a natural. Some men should be fathers," the housekeeper said pointedly, looking at Joanna.

"Mrs. Rutledge—" This was going into territory she didn't feel up to dealing with tonight.

Like a seasoned stock-car driver negotiating a track, Mrs. Rutledge effortlessly changed the course of the conversation. "There's a fresh dress for you hanging in the closet."

"Fresh dress?" Surprised, Joanna turned and looked over her shoulder toward the mirrored closet.

"Mr. Rick picked it up on his way home. If you ask me, the man's got a flair for shopping as well. Not many of those around these days." Her work here was finished. Mrs. Rutledge crossed to the doorway. "Dinner's in the dining room at six-thirty."

Still sitting on the bed, Joanna scooted back and pulled her legs up to her, encircling them with her arms as she leaned her head against her knee.

This had to be a dream, she thought. A housekeeper who doubled as a nanny, new clothes that magically appeared when she needed them. And a Prince Charming who fed and burped babies. A dream all right.

She slowly shook her head. It was tempting, so tempting to pretend that things could go back to the way they had once been.

But they couldn't. Too much had happened, too much time had gone by. You could go home again, but only to visit, not to stay.

Needing to center herself, to touch base with the reality that was her life, Joanna got up and went to see her baby.

The dress fit.

But then, she'd never doubted that it would. After

all, Rick had picked it out and he had always had an eye for color, for sizes. For everything that mattered. He was, she thought, pretty nearly perfect.

And not hers anymore. He might have saved her, might have brought her here for old times' sake, but she couldn't allow herself to confuse kindness with what they'd once had.

And didn't have anymore, she reminded herself.

As she'd slipped on the light-blue dress, the fabric felt soft and feminine against her skin. It made her feel the same.

Joanna smiled at her reflection in the mirror as she brushed her hair into place. Blond waves fell, framing her face. How was it that he always knew just what to do? Except once, of course, she amended.

But that was all in the past and it had to stay there. For both their sakes.

Ready, she tiptoed into the next room. Rachel was asleep again.

She felt a tug at her heart, seeing the baby in what had been Rick's old crib. This was the way things should have been.

But they weren't, and she should be grateful for what was, not regretful about what wasn't.

Joanna looked down at Rachel a moment longer, before stealing off. Best baby in the whole world, she thought. Of course, her first night alone was still ahead of her. That would be the real trial by fire.

So would going in and facing Rick over dinner, she thought.

The irony of the situation struck her full force. There was a time, she mused, when it wouldn't have been necessary to brace herself in order to see him.

There was a time when she would have raced into the dining room on winged feet instead of leaden ones.

"I can do this," she told herself as she left the room.

After taking one wrong turn, she found her way to the dining room. Rick was already seated, sipping a glass of wine. He rose in his chair when she entered.

"Your manners always were impeccable," she told him as she walked in.

The dining room, like the rest of the estate, was formal, with a long table designed for entertaining large parties of people. There were four tall, white tapered candles, set in silver, with flames softly teasing the air. Her place setting, she noted, was opposite his, all the way at the other end of the table. She wondered if she needed to drop bread crumbs to find her way back.

"Training," he murmured. His eyes swept over her, appreciating the silhouette she cast. If there were any remnants of her pregnancy, he certainly couldn't detect them. She was as trim as he remembered her. As trim as she appeared in his dreams. He banked down the ache he felt in his loins. "The dress looks nice on you."

As if she were bringing out the best in the dress instead of the other way around. Her mouth curved. The man had always known his way around a compliment.

Seating herself, Joanna looked down at the garment. "Thank you. Again."

"Wine?" he asked. He held his glass aloft when she didn't seem to hear. "Or are you—?"

She shook her head. "No, I'm not nursing her."

Her voice seemed to disappear into the atmosphere. She raised her voice. "Rachel's perfect in every way, but she has an allergy." She gave a small shrug. "To me, it would seem, or at least to my milk. The doctor said she's better off with a formula." She saw that he was beginning to rise and guessed at his intent. "But I'll pass on the wine right now. It'll just make me sleepy."

Although, sitting here, looking at him, was making her anything but sleepy. Anticipation seemed to be jumping through her veins, even though she knew there was nothing to anticipate.

He sat down again. Joanna toyed with her thoughts for exactly two seconds before giving voice to them. "You know, you can't just keep buying me things."

It appeared to her as if he was looking at her pointedly, although at this distance, she wasn't sure. "There was a time I would have bought you anything."

She lowered her eyes to her plate. Prime rib. Her favorite. Mrs. Rutledge had outdone herself. "And there was a time I would have let you, but right now, I'm beginning to feel like an indentured servant."

After taking another sip, Rick set down his glass. "If I recall my history correctly, the bargain was usually for seven years. Recalculating that to take in approximately two hundred and fifty years of inflation, I'd say the length of time would probably be extended to something like thirty-two years now."

Her fingers tightened around her fork. Was he saying that he wanted her in his life? No, that was only wishful thinking on her part.

"I'll pay you back in cash, if you don't mind."

Was he frowning? She certainly couldn't tell. The candles weren't giving enough illumination and the light from the chandelier had been dimmed. "I could have worn the suit you bought."

"You fell asleep in that," he pointed out. "The alternative was to have Mrs. Rutledge unearth one of my mother's dresses for you out of the attic." He knew exactly how she would have reacted to that. It was no secret that his mother had never had any use for her. "I don't think you would have wanted that."

"No, you're right." She saw him cock his head. He hadn't heard her. "I said, you're right." She frowned. "You know, I'm beginning to think I know why your parents drifted apart. It was this table. It's longer than the boundaries for Rhode Island."

Picking up the corners of her place setting, Joanna abruptly rose to her feet and slid the setting along the surface of the table until she reached the last chair directly to his right. Leaving her place setting there, she went back to retrieve her glass. She put it next to her plate and sat down triumphantly.

"There."

He'd watched her in amusement, remembering how her very presence had brought a freshness into his life that he had been utterly unaware was missing. Until she came. "I thought you might be more comfortable over there."

"I was getting hoarse over there," she contradicted. "I couldn't see your eyes from where I was sitting."

"And that's important?"

"Haven't you heard? Eyes are the windows to the soul." She realized that her eyes were smiling into his. God, but she had missed him. Missed him with every fiber of her being. It wasn't easy being noble. "Did your parents always eat like that?"

He shrugged. "When they ate together at all, yes. But most of the time they weren't even here. My father kept late hours and was away on business a great deal. My mother had her clubs, her charity work, it pretty much kept her out of the house. The only time they were here together was when they entertained." He looked around the room. It had always felt cold to him, even in the dead of summer. "I took a lot of my meals alone in here."

She could see him, a lost boy hungering for more than food at mealtimes. Something else to hold against his mother. Why did women have children if they didn't want to be with them? What organization could possibly have had a better claim to her time and her heart than her own son? "Charity begins at home."

Joanna said it with such fierceness, he had to struggle not to smile. She hadn't lost any of her feistiness, he noted. He realized that it pleased him. "My mother always thought that a very trite saying."

Joanna took a long sip of cold water, not trusting herself to answer right away. Maybe it was disrespectful to speak ill of the dead, but there was nothing about the late socialite that Joanna had liked.

"No offense, but your mother always had a way of belittling people and making them feel as if they were beneath her."

This time, he did smile. "None taken. She wasn't exactly cut out of the same cloth that Mother Teresa was." It was something he'd made his peace with as a young boy. He'd actually thought that everyone's mother was like this. Until he'd met Joanna's, and in Joanna's case, the apple hadn't fallen far from the tree. "I always envied the bond you had with your mother."

"I was lucky." Joanna smiled. Her mother was probably her favorite topic.

Her wording struck him as ironic. "Not many people would have said that—" He stopped abruptly, realizing what he'd almost said.

He was referring to her mother's circumstances. The reason his parents had come to her and said what they had. She raised her chin defensively. She wasn't ashamed of who she was.

"In my place?" she guessed, concluding his thought. "Why, because my father did the proverbial disappearing act right after my mother told him she was pregnant? Because my mother had to raise me alone?"

The scenario had been so classic, but she still ached for her mother whenever she thought about it. Her mother had been seventeen and afraid, but, she'd assured Joanna, she'd loved her from the first moment she knew she was carrying her.

When Joanna had been a great deal younger, she'd fantasized that her father would just show up one day, begging their forgiveness. He'd ask her to be a flower girl at their wedding. When Joanna was nine, her mother had heard from a friend of a friend that her father had died in an automobile accident, and that was the end of that fantasy.

But even though she'd had no father, she counted herself extremely lucky to have had her mother in her life. Besides, what if her father had turned out to be a man like Rick's father? She was convinced she was better off this way.

There was no way Rick wanted Joanna to think that he pitied her. Nothing could have been further from the truth.

"No, I was just commenting on the fact that you always saw the glass as half full and about to be filled to the top no matter what. I always thought that was one of your best attributes."

"That, too, was a gift from my mother." Her mother had been the most upbeat person she'd ever known. And she'd always liked Rick, Joanna remembered. "A positive attitude is what gets you through life."

Rick nodded. He could remember sitting in Joanna's kitchen, hearing her mother saying that. He looked at Joanna. "How long…?"

When he hesitated, she knew what he was asking. "Has she been gone? A little over thirteen months."

The loss of Joanna's mother filled him with a great deal more sadness than the loss of his own had. "I'm sorry she couldn't have lived to see her namesake."

That was probably her biggest regret, Joanna thought. That her mother wasn't there to share all these things with her. She saw motherhood from a whole new perspective now that she was one. There was so much she would have wanted to tell her mother.

"Yes, me too."

He had to ask. "Why did you decide to have a baby now?"

It had come to her one evening, sitting alone in her

empty house. "Well, after my mother died, I just felt I needed someone to love. I had all this love to give, and there was no one around to take it. So, I decided to have a baby."

He could understand that part of it easily enough, it was the way she went about it that didn't make any sense to him. It wasn't as if Joanna was hearing her biological clock ticking loud and clear. She was only twenty-eight. There was plenty of time left.

"Why that way, though? Most women would have tried to find the right man first."

There was no point to that. She raised her eyes to his. "I'd already found him."

Was she trying to tell him there'd been someone else in her life? That she'd broken it off with someone else as well? "Who?"

Sometimes, she decided, men could be very, very dense. Even intelligent ones. "Fishing for a compliment? You, you idiot."

The words came out before he could stop them. "If that was true, then why did you do what you did?"

There it was, the white elephant in the dining room. They'd acknowledged its presence. She supposed it had to come to that sometime.

She looked away. The terrain was painful, even after all this time. She supposed it always would be. "I did it for you."

"For me?" he echoed.

His tone was cynical and it rankled her. Anger rose up in her chest. "Well, I didn't do it for me. It was the hardest thing I'd ever done."

"Was it? Was ripping out my heart really hard for

you? Or did accepting the bribe make you forget all about that part of it?''

"Bribe?" Her appetite gone, she pushed her plate away. "What bribe? What the hell are you talking about?''

He could taste his anger as it rose up in his throat. All those years, wasted, because she didn't believe in him, didn't believe that he could rise above anything his father threw his way and take care of both of them. "Don't act dumb, Joanna, it doesn't become you."

She drew herself up, her eyes flashing. All the emotion that had been pent up for so long threatened to come pouring out. "Don't you dare tell me how to act. I can be dumb if I want to, especially when I have no idea what you're talking about."

She was lying to him. After all this time, she was lying. How could she? Didn't she think he knew? "My father told me all about it."

She just bet he did. Joanna crossed her arms before her. "Enlighten me. *What* did he tell you?"

He had the urge just to get up and walk away. And keep walking.

But he'd done that once and it had brought him back here. This time, he was going to confront her, get it all out. And defy her to talk her way out of it.

"That he told you if you married me, he'd disown me and there wouldn't be a penny for us, but that if you left me, he'd give you a check for fifty thousand dollars. And you took the money."

Joanna's mouth dropped open. Did he actually believe that? "I did what?"

"You took the money," he repeated. It took effort

not to shout at her, not to demand to know why she'd thrown everything away like that. "I saw the check with your endorsement on the back. I refused to believe it until then, until he showed me the proof."

For a second, Joanna was just too stunned to speak. It never occurred to her that people would go to such lengths to pull off a deception. Never occurred to her because she would have never done anything like that herself. She didn't believe in lying.

Shaking her head, she blew out a breath. "I guess your father can add forgery to his list of talents. Forgery as well as lying."

"You're telling me it never happened?" It was a challenge, even though he knew better.

Her eyes held his for a very long moment. "I'm telling you that not all of it happened. Yes, your parents came to me, and yes they told me that if I married you, they'd disown you. And yes, there was an offer of a check." Her eyes darkened. "But that's where the story changes. I tore the check up in front of them. That was when your mother took me aside and painted a very vivid scenario of how you would grow to hate me because you had to face an existence without all the things you were accustomed to. And that it would be because of me."

It was his turn to stare at her, not knowing whether or not to believe what she was saying. "And you believed her?"

Joanna sighed. Angry tears rose in her eyes at the memory.

"I didn't want to, but she was very, very persuasive and I was afraid that there was more than just a germ of truth in what she was saying. I could live with struggling to make our way in the world, I'd done it all my life. But I didn't know if you could and I didn't think it was right for me to be the one to deprive you of all your 'creature comforts,' as your mother put it.''

Suddenly the walls were down and it was eight years ago. She had to tell him now what she couldn't have told him then. ''I would rather have died than to have you hate me. And in a way, I guess I did.''

''You never took the money,'' he repeated slowly, letting the words sink in.

''I never took the money.'' Why did she have to convince him? He'd loved her once, how could he not believe in her? ''You want to hook me up to a lie detector?'' she asked cynically.

He swallowed an angry retort. ''Why didn't you come to tell me all this?''

He should have known the answer to this, too. ''Because if I came to you, I *wouldn't* have been able to tell you all this. You wouldn't have let me walk away.'' *And even if you had, I wouldn't have been able to.*

''Damn right I wouldn't have.''

''And every day, I would have lived in fear of seeing you slowly begin to resent me, then hate me.''

Rick couldn't believe she was saying this. ''Didn't you know me any better than that?''

Joanna shrugged. Maybe she should have trusted him, maybe she should have trusted herself. But his mother had been so confident....

''I thought I did, but I didn't want to risk it. I was twenty years old and, by your parents' standards, very naive. You meant the world to me and I wanted you to be happy.''

He'd been everything but that. "So you left me.''

''So I left you,'' she echoed. It had been the single most unselfish thing she'd ever done and it had almost killed her. "Your parents said that Loretta Langley was much better suited for you.''

He remembered his parents' efforts to push the two of them together right after his father had dropped the bombshell about Joanna taking the bribe. "Loretta Langley was a shallow, narcissistic cardboard figure my mother could easily lead around by the nose. I didn't want a puppet, I wanted you.''

Tears burned her eyes. She blinked them back. ''Then why didn't you try to come after me? Why did you just pick up and leave?''

''Because I was hurt.''

His parents had done a stellar job of ruining two lives, she thought. "Because you believed I could be bought. How could you?''

He answered her question with one of his own. ''How could you believe that I'd actually pick my empty lifestyle over you?''

''I guess your father's a better salesman than either of us ever thought.'' She laughed shortly.

He couldn't believe it. All those years lost because of lies. "So now what?''

Too much time had gone by for them to pick up where they'd left off, she thought, even though she wished it was otherwise. There were things to resolve, trust to rebuild. Once it was lost, trust was a very hard thing to find again. It was like learning how to walk again after a car accident had denied you the use of your legs.

Maybe, eventually...

"Now we finish our meal," Joanna proposed, moving her plate back in front of her, "and take it one step at a time." Her eyes widened as Rick abruptly stood up. The legs of his chair scraped loudly along the marble floor. "What are you doing?"

Taking hold of her wrist, Rick brought her to her feet and pulled her to him. "I've just decided what I want my first step to be."

Six

She didn't get a chance to ask "What?"

The question was unnecessary anyway.

She knew.

One look into his eyes and Joanna knew. He wanted exactly what she wanted, what she'd thought about, dreamed about these last long years without him.

Rick dove his fingers through her hair, tilting her face up to his. Bringing his mouth down to hers.

The torrent of emotion, secured behind dams that had been weakening these last few days broke loose, flooding both of them.

Oh, but she'd missed this, missed him.

Wrapping her arms around his neck, Joanna pressed her body against his, absorbing that old, familiar heat and reveling in it as it shot through her at the speed of Mach 8.

Who said you couldn't recapture the past, at least for a moment? Kissing Rick erased all the years, all the heartache. She was twenty again, and in love.

Desire surged through him with a vengeance that all but rattled his teeth. She still had the power to weaken his knees and reduce him to a pile of needy ashes in the space of a few seconds. No other woman could ever do that. No other woman even came close.

But then, he'd never loved anyone but her. The others who populated his social life were there due to sheer physical attraction alone, an attraction that quickly waned, leaving as abruptly as it came. Once he slept with a woman, the pull was no longer there. He was, he knew, subconsciously searching for someone to take Joanna's place.

But this, this was different. It always had been. The more he kissed her, the more he wanted to kiss her.

If there was such a thing as a soul mate, then Joanna had been his. Once.

Desire slammed into him, demanding release, demanding that he act on it. But even if there wasn't Joanna's condition to think of, this was too soon. He felt it in his bones.

You couldn't recapture the past and turn it into the present just because you wanted to.

Could you?

Logic disintegrated, leaving only rubble in its wake. All that remained was need.

Rick could feel every fiber of his body wanting her. In another moment, he wasn't sure if he could rein himself in.

Pulling his head back, he framed her face with his hands and looked at her.

"Damn, but you still have the ability to knock my shoes off."

She glanced down at his feet and then raised her eyes to his. "Figuratively speaking." Her mouth curved as she tried very hard not to tremble.

His own smile faded. He wanted her so badly, he was surprised that he didn't go up in smoke.

"How long?" he asked. She cocked her head and looked at him, confused. "How long before you're able to make love with me?"

Her smile, so reminiscent of the girl he'd once known, went straight to his heart. "Cutting right to the chase?"

His throat felt dry. "It's been eight years, Joey, there's no cutting to anything."

Joey. It was a nickname only he used. It brought back a flood of memories. She could almost feel him whispering it against her ear as they lay in one another's arms, enshrouded in darkness and the contented afterglow of lovemaking.

She closed her eyes as he pressed a kiss to her throat. Wishing she could go back and change things. Wishing that they hadn't lost all the time that they had.

Joanna shivered as desire teased her very core. She opened her eyes and looked up at him. "Soon, I hope. Very soon. The doctor said I was making great progress and there weren't any complications. I've heard some women can do it as soon as two weeks after they give birth. And I've always been very, very healthy."

He brushed the hair from her face, reluctant to let her go. "Two weeks," he murmured.

"It might be longer," she cautioned.

"It already is." He brushed a kiss to her forehead, holding her to him for a moment longer. He felt his body quickening, rebelling against his resolve. But he'd been without her all this time, he could wait a little longer. From a safe distance.

Dropping his arms to his sides, Rick took a step back, then moved his chair into place. If he didn't leave now, he wasn't sure if he could keep from touching her.

Was he leaving? In the middle of dinner? "Where are you going?"

"To take a long, cold shower. I've got a feeling I'm going to be taking a lot of them in the next couple of weeks. Or longer," he tacked on.

Turning to leave, Rick suddenly swung around again. His hand against the column of her throat, tilting her head back, he pressed a quick, deep kiss to her lips. One for the road. "I'll see you tomorrow."

"Tomorrow?" She looked down at his plate. He'd only half finished his meal.

Rick nodded. "It's going to be a very long shower." He nodded at her plate. "You'd better finish that or Mrs. Rutledge is going to take it as a personal insult. She tells me she spent a lot of time preparing your favorite meal."

She didn't have much of an appetite. He'd stirred things up in her, making her ache for him. "You didn't finish yours," she pointed out.

He laughed shortly. "She's used to that." And then he winked at her. "Besides, I've got a feeling you'd better build up your strength."

With that, he turned and walked out of the dining room, leaving her to her meal. And some very erotic thoughts.

By the time Rick stepped out of the onyx-tiled shower, he felt almost waterlogged. He'd remained in the enclosure for a very long time, not only trying to cool off desires that felt almost insurmountable, but also to try to get a handle on his anger. Anger against his parents and especially his father. The sense of betrayal was almost overwhelming.

Had it only been his mother who had come to him with the story of bribery, he would have been highly skeptical and far more inclined to get to the bottom of it himself. He knew his mother didn't approve of Joanna, that she had set her sights on his marrying "within his class," whatever the hell that was supposed to mean.

But his father was another matter. His father had always kept clear of his mother's machinations. He rubber-stamped a lot of things, ignored others. Rick had the feeling that his father might have even liked Joanna, at least a little. He'd never echoed his mother's feelings about her, never looked down on Joanna because her family weren't "people of substance." So when the man had backed up his mother and even produced the endorsed check, Rick had felt he had no choice but to believe that Joanna had been bought off.

He'd thought they'd gotten somewhat closer these last couple of years, he and his father, shedding the roles of two strangers. He'd been at his father's side right after the heart attack.

So why hadn't he told him about his deception?

Was everything in his life a lie?

It was hard for Rick not to feel bitter.

Getting out of the shower, he toweled his hair furiously as he crossed to the telephone next to his bed. He tossed the towel aside and hit the speed dial for his father's cell phone.

It rang twenty times before the metallic voice came on to tell him that his father was either out of the area, or not picking up.

"No kidding, Sherlock," Rick muttered.

He hurried into his clothes, then, his hair still wet, Rick went downstairs to his office. He kept a phone book there of all the important numbers he might need. Taking the book out of the top drawer in his desk, he flipped through it and found the phone number to his father's house in Florida.

It was past eleven on the east coast, but this matter wasn't going to wait until morning. It had waited long enough.

Rick heard the answering machine pick up. Frustration flooded him as he waited for the short, utilitarian message to be over. "Dad, if you're around, pick up. You there, Dad? Pick up, it's important."

Nothing. Muttering a curse, Rick had begun to hang up when he heard a noise on the other end of the line.

"Hello? Richard? Is that you? What's wrong? Something happen to the negotiations for the new headquarters?"

Jerking the receiver back to his ear, Rick's fingers tightened around it.

"What's wrong?" he echoed, barely keeping his

fury in check. "I'll tell you what's wrong, old man. You lied to me."

There was an uneasy pause on the other end. "Richard? Have you been drinking?"

Rick dragged his hand through his wet hair, pacing back and forth around his desk. "No, I haven't been drinking. I also haven't been seeing things clearly, either."

"I don't understand."

"Neither do I." He blew out an angry breath. Damn it, he'd thought he could at least trust his own father. "I could see why Mother would have lied to me. She always wanted things her way, wanted to control my every move just the way she did yours. But you, Dad, you forged that check and made me believe something that tore me apart. Didn't you give even a small damn about me?"

There was another long pause on the other end.

"How did you find out?" Howard asked as he realized it was finally over, finally out in the open. The subject was one that had never been completely buried for Howard Masters, even though he'd tried to put it out of his mind over the years. It felt as if a huge weight had been lifted from his shoulders.

Rick was surprised that there wasn't even the vaguest attempt at denial on his father's part. He didn't know whether that made him angrier, or relieved that he was finally going to confess.

"I did what I should have done eight years ago. I talked to her."

Howard Masters had been preparing himself for this ever since he'd made the suggestion that the home office be moved from Georgia. It had been his way of orchestrating things. ''I'm glad it's out in the open.'' He only hoped his son believed him.

''Glad, are you?'' Rick sincerely doubted that. He struggled to keep his voice down. If he started shouting, he knew Mrs. Rutledge would hear him. Though she was more family to him than either of his parents ever were, he didn't want to bring her into this. ''Then why the hell didn't you tell me yourself? These last couple of years when we were working together, why didn't you say something?''

''I tried. More than a few times.'' His conscience had kept goading him to tell Rick. ''But things got in the way.''

''What things?'' Rick demanded. What could possibly have kept his father from telling him the truth after his mother was gone?

''Business.'' Howard hesitated, then told him the truth. ''Cowardice, I suppose. We were getting closer and I valued that. I didn't want to risk losing you. And before that, there was your mother to reckon with.'' Opening that can of worms would have caused an even greater schism in the family.

That was a poor excuse. ''Mother's been dead for three years.''

''You seemed to be happy with your new life,'' his father said lamely.

''Happy?'' he demanded. ''Dad, I've never been happy a day in my life, except when I was with Joanna.''

''If it means anything, I'm sorry.'' Howard sighed. ''Ever since the heart attack, I really have been trying to find a way to tell you. I decided the best way was to make you come back to Bedford for more than four hours. I knew Joanna still lived there. I was hoping circumstances might bring you together.''

Some of the anger left. Rick realized that his father had deliberately decided to move company headquarters out of Georgia. His father had insisted on it, even when Rick had balked and said it wasn't a good idea. His protest had been drowned in a sea of statistics his father had sent to him showing why the move was advantageous.

Rick dropped into his chair and tilted it back. ''This doesn't get you off the hook, you know.''

''I know. That'll take time. I hope I'll have it.''

In the last year, his father had come face-to-face with his own mortality and no longer took for granted that he had an infinite amount of time. It was a far cry from the man who'd once acted as if he was going to live forever.

Rick thought he heard a woman's voice in the background, calling his father's name. ''Who's that?''

''Someone who's made me realize more clearly that I should have never stood in the way of your happiness, no matter how convinced your mother was that it didn't lie with that girl.''

''She has a name, Dad. Joanna.'' Rick paused. It had never occurred to him that his father might find someone. The relationship with his mother had been such a failure, he would have thought that would have stopped his father from ever venturing out on the field again. ''What's the name of the woman with you?''

''Dorothy.'' Rick could hear a smile in his father's voice as he said the name. ''Richard, maybe someday you can find it in your heart to forgive me.''

''Yeah, maybe.''

But not now, not yet. It was going to take him time to work through this. Time to resolve everything in his life. It was the second time that his parents had upended everything for him, and it was going to take a while before things could get back to some semblance of normalcy.

"We'll talk later." He didn't trust himself to say anything further right now.

Rick replaced the receiver. He sat, staring at the telephone for a long time.

The sound of crying roused him. Rick realized that he must have dozed off. Small wonder. Going over quarterly reports was guaranteed to put anyone to sleep. He'd sought refuge in work the way he always did when his thoughts began to crowd in on him. Once, when he'd left Bedford for the east coast, it had been his saving grace.

His mouth felt like cotton. Rick stretched, his muscles aching from sleeping in an easy chair. The thick binder that had been on his lap slipped to the floor. He bent over to pick it up.

The crying got louder.

The baby was crying. Joanna's baby.

Joanna.

He nearly stumbled as he got up. Rick tossed the binder onto his desk and left the room, stopping only to shut off the light behind him.

Making his way to the rear of the house, he knocked on Joanna's door, the wonder of everything seeping into his system all over again. She was here, in his house, with a child, after all this time. There was happiness, but there was a sense of unrest as well, that he couldn't quite banish.

It was all new, he counseled himself. He had to give himself time.

When there was no answer, he tried the doorknob. The door wasn't locked. He opened it slowly, not wanting to intrude, but wanting to be there for her if she needed him. Wanting her to know he was there. Because of pain and altruism, they'd both hurt each other before. He wanted her to know that somehow, things would be right this time. This was one of the small steps in getting there. Helping her out in this new position she found herself in.

He saw her standing by the window, moonlight and a small night-light from the other room mingling to create a surreal atmosphere in the room. She was wearing the nightgown he'd gotten her, and he could feel his gut twisting at the sight of her.

The black nightgown was far from practical, made of lace, nylon and unfulfilled dreams. The light from the moon was thrusting its way through the material, highlighting her body just enough to make him ache. Just enough to make him remember.

Her hair was loose about her shoulders, tousled as if she'd just gotten out of bed. He longed to run his hands through it, through it and over her, reclaiming what had once been his.

Maybe he should leave, he thought, before she saw him standing there.

But she was holding the baby to her, trying to soothe her. Mother and baby both looked distressed.

"What's wrong?"

She turned, startled. She hadn't heard him come in.

Her attention had been completely focused on the baby. "I didn't mean to wake you."

He smiled, crossing to her. "You didn't. The baby did."

She still thought of them as a unit, she and the baby. Or maybe she wasn't thinking clearly at all. She'd had a nightmare just before Rachel's crying had woken her. A nightmare in which Rick's parents were surrounding her, larger than life and saying over and over again that she wasn't good enough for their son, that loving her would only bring him down. After all these years, she supposed a part of her still believed that.

"Sorry."

"Don't be sorry." He looked at the tiny wailing human being scrunched up against her chest. "How long has she been fussing?"

"A while now." She'd done all the right things, why wasn't Rachel going back to sleep? She'd been so good up until now.

Had she done something wrong?

Joanna looked tired, he thought. He brushed her hair back from her face. "Want me to get Mrs. Rutledge?"

"No." The word came out more fiercely than she'd intended. She lowered her voice. "Rachel is my responsibility. What kind of a mother would I be, handing her off to a nanny every time she made a sound or needed something?"

His mother, he thought, but kept the response to himself. Joanna wasn't anything like his mother and making the comparison would only upset her. So instead, he said, "A mother who knows how to accept help."

She was tired and frustrated, but it was something she was going to have to learn how to deal with. Her mother used to have a saying. No one ever fell from heaven pre-taught. That went for mothers, too.

"Mrs. Rutledge has been helping ever since I walked through the door. She deserves to sleep."

"So do you." He looked at the fussing infant. "Did you change her?"

"Of course I changed her." She realized she was snapping and amended her tone. "Sorry. I fed her, too."

"Then maybe all she needs is to be rocked a little." He held out his hands. "Here, give her to me."

She hesitated. She so wanted to do this right. "But it's late, you should be in bed."

He lifted a shoulder, letting it drop carelessly. "Nobody to be there with. I could stand a little companionship." Not waiting for Joanna to give him the infant, he took the baby from her. "Here, I won't drop her. I'm the one who held her first, remember?"

Reluctantly, she surrendered Rachel to him. She would never have thought he would want to bother himself with a baby. It made her realize that there was a lot about him she still didn't know. "Mrs. Rutledge told me you fed her earlier."

He smiled down at the bundle in his arms. "Mrs. Rutledge talks too much."

"She dotes on you, you know."

"The feeling's mutual." He sat down in the rocking chair in the corner and nodded toward the bed. "Why don't you lie down for a while? I'll take over."

"You don't have to do this." Even as she protested, Joanna sat down on the bed and slid back. "I mean, it's not as if you were her father."

His eyes met hers across the room. "No, but I could have been, if I believed in making donations. Don't argue with me. Lie down."

"Just for a second," she murmured.

It was the last thing she said. She fell asleep watching Rick rock the baby in the chair where Mrs. Rutledge had once sat, rocking him.

The last thought she had before she drifted off was that it was nice to have traditions in your life.

Seven

Rick's cell phone rang just as he was hurrying into his car. In deference to his position as vice president of Masters Enterprises, he was driving his Mercedes rather than his beloved Mustang.

It was a compromise. His father had wanted him to use the chauffeur-driven limousines, the way he had. The senior Masters maintained that it was more fitting. But Rick preferred being in the driver's seat himself. Preferred being in control. He supposed he got that from his mother. He considered it the only positive link between them.

He put his key into the ignition, then pulled the cell phone out of his pocket. Flipping it open, he paused before starting the car. "Masters."

"Mr. Rick, it's Nadine Rutledge."

There was no need to introduce herself. No one else

called him Mr. Rick or had quite that soft, Southern lilt in her voice.

Apprehension tightened his stomach. The last time he had heard from Mrs. Rutledge via telephone, it had been to inform him that his mother had died. His first thoughts were of Joanna and the baby.

"What's wrong?"

As always, Mrs. Rutledge's voice was low-key, soothing. "I'm not all that sure whether something is wrong, Mr. Rick, but Miss Joanna left."

"Left?" Echoes of the past came hurdling at him. Mrs. Rutledge couldn't mean that Joanna had left permanently. "Left where? Where did she go?"

"To her house, or what's left of it."

Relief was short-lived. What could Joanna have been thinking, going there now? He'd already given her a report on the condition of her house, brought her purse to her with her credit cards and wallet in it. Why this sudden need to go? Or, if she had to see it for herself, why hadn't she at least waited for him to get home?

"Did you try to stop her?"

It was evident by her voice that although Mrs. Rutledge was the one who ran everything in the house and had done so for his father after his mother's death, she didn't feel that it was her position to deter Joanna physically from doing what she wanted.

"I told her she shouldn't be doing this, but she insisted. I gave her my cell phone." It was clearly her way of compromising.

Frustration waltzed through him. Had Joanna taken his car? "Is she even supposed to be driving yet?"

He vaguely recalled Joanna saying that her doctor had warned her against it.

"That just pertains to a week after delivery. It's been almost two weeks," Mrs. Rutledge reminded him. "But she's not driving, she took a cab there."

"Damn it," he muttered. Exasperated, he glanced at his watch. He was meeting with the architect for the new home office in half an hour. Well, that was just going to have to wait. Joanna's well-being was more important than steel girders and Doric columns. "Do me a favor. Call my office and tell Celia to reschedule my meeting with Donnelley and Sons. Have her tell them something came up and I'll see them at their office this afternoon at two."

"Consider it done."

"I already do."

Ending the conversation, Rick flipped the phone closed. He tossed it on the seat next to him, not bothering to waste time putting it away.

He couldn't help wondering what was going on in Joanna's head. Damn it, why was she doing this to herself? Seeing everything she loved destroyed would only be hard on her.

He turned the key in the ignition and pulled out of his parking spot. She'd been so busy this last week and a half, learning her way around this new phase of her life. Learning to be a mother. He'd thought that, beyond making an appointment with her insurance agent for sometime later in the week, Joanna had put the fire and its consequences out of her mind. At least temporarily.

Apparently not.

Just showed him he had no idea what went on in her head. He didn't know if he liked that or not.

For the last week and a half, despite the fact that Masters Enterprises was an international corporation and that if he was going to remain a hands-on leader, there was enough work to keep him busy around the clock, he found himself ending his days early. Coming home just to share the experience of parenting with Joanna, or watching quietly from the sidelines, absorbing the essence of mother and daughter.

When he'd seriously thought of their future while they'd been going together, it had never really included this phase of it. He'd envisioned the two of them flying to exotic locations, making love in all four corners of the world. Attending the elegant parties that were so much a part of his world. Enjoying life and each other. Alive with excitement. The thought of babies had only remotely entered into the scenario. Babies meant tedium, his parents had taught him that.

But babies weren't tedious. They represented a completely new, completely different kind of excitement. One marked with joy. And although he tried not to give it too much thought, sharing his days with Rachel and Joanna was bringing him in, centering him in a way he'd never thought he'd be centered.

He didn't want just to be a spectator, he wanted to be part of it all.

Was it the newness that was pulling him in like this? The feeling of recapturing the past in a whole new, different way? Would this exhilarating feeling and his involvement ultimately fade as he became accustomed to what was going on?

Rick turned down the next street, away from the building. He didn't try to fool himself. He was a different man than he'd been eight years ago. He'd grown in different directions, grown without Joanna at his side. She'd grown as well. He'd only had to look at this turn of events and her choice of single parenthood to know that she had.

Could the two halves fit together again, after all these years?

He didn't know.

What he did know was that rooting around in the ashes of what had been her home since childhood couldn't be good for her.

Rick pushed down harder on the accelerator, going faster as he kept an eye out for any police cars that might suddenly appear behind him.

Speed had never been particularly alluring to him. He ordinarily kept within the legal ranges without giving it much thought. But he found himself having to ease back on the accelerator now, flying through lights that were about to turn from yellow to red.

He made it across town to her development in record time.

Approaching her block, he could still detect a very faint smell of smoke even after all this time.

Or was that just his imagination?

His imagination had never been a particularly vivid one, except whenever Joanna entered into the picture. Everything that had to do with her was amplified, always just a little larger than life,

There was no sign of a cab on the block.

Maybe Mrs. Rutledge had been mistaken. Maybe Joanna had just gone to meet one of her friends for an early lunch, or decided to go shopping for clothes. She'd absolutely forbidden him to buy her any more things. Maybe she'd decided to replenish her nonexistent wardrobe on her own.

And then he saw her.

He'd almost missed her because she was down on her knees, sifting through charred ashes. Pulling up at the curb, Rick quickly shut off the ignition and jumped out of the car. Joanna gave no indication that she even knew he was there. Wrapped in her thoughts, she seemed to be completely oblivious to everything outside of the circle immediately around her.

For a moment, he thought of just leaving her with her thoughts and waiting until she rose and turned around.

But the sight of her form, so obviously enshrouded in grief even from the back, moved him so incredibly, he could feel tears of his own gathering in his eyes. She shouldn't have to be going through this. No one should.

Very softly, he came up behind her, not wanting to intrude, not wanting her to go through this alone.

"Joanna?"

Startled, she turned and looked over her shoulder. Her face was stained with tears.

The hell with standing back and giving her room to grieve. He erased the last few steps between them as he hurried to her. Crouching, he took her into his arms and raised her to her feet.

"Oh God, Joanna, why did you come here?"

She wasn't going to cry anymore, she wasn't, she told herself fiercely.

"I had to." She tried very hard to sound flippant. "I knew the mailbox had to be getting full." She nodded toward the structure at the curb, a cheery-looking miniature of the house that had once been whole. The mailbox was completely untouched by the tragedy that was behind it. She'd had it made as a gift to her mother one Easter. "I never left a forwarding address for the mail carrier," she explained with a slight shrug of her shoulder.

He framed her face with his hands and kissed her lightly. It had never even occurred to him to come by and check for mail, or to arrange for the mail to be delivered to his house. He'd see to it immediately. "I should have thought of that."

She shook her head, drawing away. Part of her was rebelling, calling herself weak for not standing on her own two feet. For leaning on someone, even if it was Rick. She was supposed to be stronger than that. She had to be strong because life had a way of running you down if you weren't.

"You've been thinking of everything else." She looked at him almost defiantly. "You're not responsible for me, Rick."

He took her hand, stopping her from moving away. "But I want to be."

She couldn't give up her independence, even to him. "I'm not fragile, Rick. I can take care of myself." And then she bit her lower lip as a fresh wave of tears came to her, threatening to undo everything she'd just said. "They're all gone."

He wasn't sure he knew what she was referring to. "What's all gone? Memories?" he guessed. "They're still there in your head, Joey.'' Lightly, he touched her temple. ''They always will be.''

She pressed her lips together. He undid her resolve by calling her Joey. She blinked hard to keep the dam inside from bursting, to keep the tears from washing over her face again. She didn't want to cry, she wanted to be strong. Had to be strong.

But so much had happened in her life this last year and a half. First her mother's illness, then her death. Then the board politely telling her she was an embarrassment and letting her go. And now part of her house was taken away from her. It was as if she couldn't be allowed to hold onto anything.

Was it always going to be that way? It made her afraid to rely on anything, least of all happiness.

''My photographs are all gone.'' Her voice was shaky and she paused to gather her strength to her. ''My mother's albums were stored in the living room and I found those. But the ones of us…'' She looked up at him, trying to remember him the way he was the first time she'd seen him. His hair was far more unruly and longer then. And there'd been a rebelliousness about him that time had taken away. ''The ones of you…were in my bedroom closet.''

She looked back at what had once been the rear of the house. It was hard even to pinpoint where the closet had been. That half of the house was now just a blackened shell, its frame barely standing.

He didn't know what to say, how to comfort her. He knew what photographs meant to her. When they'd begun going together, she'd insisted on snapping pictures almost constantly, capturing moments and freezing them for all time.

"Where are your mother's albums?" he asked.

Rather than answer, she took him by the hand and led him into the house. It felt funny, being able to enter through what had once been the dining room.

Joanna stopped at a large maple hutch that had sustained some smoke damage, but for the most part, was untouched by the fire. She opened the bottom doors. There were at least fifteen albums nestled against one another, arranged by years.

Seeing them, Rick couldn't help but smile. "She was a very orderly person."

"Yes, she was." Joanna's voice caught in her throat. And then she saw him begin to remove the albums one by one. "What are you doing?"

"I'm going to take them back with us. Bedford isn't known for having looters, but you can never be too safe with something as precious as these."

She knew he was saying that for her benefit, that he didn't care about photographs himself. He'd told her he never kept any. She brushed a kiss against his cheek. "Thank you."

It took three trips to move the albums from the hutch to the trunk of his car. He left the lid open. "Anything else?"

Joanna turned to look at the house. It reminded her of an illustration she'd once seen of Dr. Jekyll and Mr. Hyde. Half stately, half grotesque. "Everything," she replied with a heavy sigh.

He wasn't sure if she was kidding, but this was Joanna. He was willing to humor her. "We could come back with a truck."

With a small laugh, she shook her head. "I wasn't being serious, just sad. The photographs are the most important thing. That," she turned toward the mailbox, her mouth curving with self depreciating humor, "and the bills."

Crossing to it, she opened the small door, trying not to think of anything at all. She emptied the mailbox and placed the contents on the floor behind the passenger seat in the car. She didn't bother sorting through the large pile. She'd deal with all that later.

Rick was right beside her. "Where's the cab, by the way?"

"I sent the cab away. I didn't know how long I was going to be here and I couldn't afford to have the driver standing there with the meter running."

That sounded almost flighty, especially for her. "How did you plan to get back?"

Reaching into her pocket, she pulled out a cell phone and held it up. "Mrs. Rutledge gave me her phone so I thought I'd call a cab when I was done feeling sorry for myself." She put it back in her pocket.

Rick slipped his arm around her shoulders, drawing her closer to him, mutely giving her support. It meant the world to her, even though she told herself not to become dependent on it.

"You weren't feeling sorry for yourself, Joanna," he told her. "You grew up in this house. You have every right to grieve because part of it was destroyed."

For a moment, she let him protect her from everything. Let him make it all right. Turning her head against his arm, she looked up at him. "When did you get to be so sensitive?" The old Rick had been sweet and loving, but this was a level of compassion she wasn't familiar with.

"There's this program they have at work," he teased. "They make me take it for my own good." He brushed his lips against her forehead. "Ready to go home? Or do you need a little more time?"

She'd gotten everything she'd come for. "No, I don't need more time. You're right. What's most important is in here," she tapped her forehead the way he'd done earlier.

And in here, she added, thinking of her heart. A heart that was filled with love for her baby.

And for him.

But something kept her from voicing her feelings, a small, undefined fear that made her believe that things were not the way they had once been. They couldn't be. They weren't the same people they'd been then and she had come to learn not to expect anything.

When you didn't expect things, you weren't disappointed.

Holding the passenger door open for her, Rick picked up his cell phone from the seat and helped her into the car. He rounded the hood and got in behind the steering wheel. Strapping in, he glanced at his watch. With his meeting pushed back, he had some time on his hands. Returning to the office held no appeal to him. The work could wait.

Inspiration came out of nowhere. It had been a long time since he'd done anything on the spur of the moment. Rick started the car and pulled away from the curb. "Do you feel like going shopping?"

She stopped watching the house get smaller in the side mirror. "What?"

He took a right turn at the end of the block. "I seem to remember an old saying or joke that went 'Whenever I'm down in the dumps, I go shopping.' I thought there might be a kernel of truth in it." He was hoping that doing something familiar like that might cheer her up a little. "You do need more clothes, you know. Three outfits do not a wardrobe make."

She knew he meant well, but this had to stop. She wasn't his mistress, to be showered with gifts. He'd found her credit cards for her, but she was saving those for living expenses.

"I thought I told you not to buy me anything else."

"You did," he said matter-of-factly. Rick slanted her a look before making another right turn, this time onto a major street that led out of the development. "I take lousy instructions. Besides, I won't be picking them out this time, you will be. How about it?" When she didn't respond immediately, he asked, "Tired?"

"No, not at all." She'd been feeling more energetic lately. The baby hadn't learned how to sleep any longer, but she'd developed a pattern of being able to manage on less sleep herself. "But I really should be getting back to Rachel."

If that was the only reason, they were in the clear. "Don't worry about that. Mrs. Rutledge is having a ball with her. I'll just call her and tell her that you're all right and that we'll be a couple of hours late. She called me. She was worried," he explained, answering the silent question in her eyes.

"That explains what you were doing here." She

was seriously beginning to entertain the idea that he just materialized every time she needed him.

Shopping. Why not? Maybe something a little more normal might be in order after all. And this way, if she was there, she could keep a lid on the spending.

"All right," Joanna agreed impulsively, leaning back in her seat, "let's go shopping."

She felt like Cinderella.

Or maybe it was Julia Roberts in *Pretty Woman* she was thinking of. Whatever the comparison, Rick was making her feel like a princess.

Warning her ahead of time that he would leave her stranded in the middle of Los Angeles National Forest if she uttered a single negative word about cost, Rick took her to several exclusive shops in Newport Beach. With an unfailing eye, he selected just the right clothes for her, both casual and elegant, turning a deaf ear to her protests that all she needed before she was on her own was perhaps just a couple more *simple* items.

Since money had never been an obstacle in his life, Rick spent it as if it meant nothing. Joanna couldn't help thinking that he was every woman's dream when it came to generosity.

When it came to other things as well, but she wasn't going to allow herself to go there. If she didn't dream, she insisted silently, she wouldn't feel deprived when she woke up.

She had to all but drag him out of the third store before he bought her a complete wardrobe. The only thing that stopped him was that he had to be getting back to work.

Boxes and shopping bags had joined the pile of mail in the back seat, threatening to overflow into the front.

"I'm keeping a tally on this, you know," she informed him as she got into the car. She pulled her seatbelt around her, buckling up. "And at this rate, I'm going to have to turn over my next three years' salary to you."

Provided she could talk the board into taking her back now that her rounded abdomen was no longer a source of embarrassment to them, she thought.

He didn't want to hear about payback. "Joanna, let me make you a present of them."

It was too much and he knew it. "There's a difference between getting a present and buying a whole person," she pointed out.

He smiled as he guided the car back onto MacArthur Boulevard. "If you're determined to make some kind of payment," he glanced at her, "we could work it out in the barter system."

Tiny pinpricks of anticipation traveled through her. "What kind of barter system?"

His smile broadened considerably. "I'll think of something."

That they were going to make love was a foregone conclusion. But that had nothing to do with her owing him for all these things that he had insisted on doing for her. She prided herself on always paying her own way.

"It's going to be nothing less than cash and carry," she informed him.

He winked at her before looking back at the road. "We'll talk."

She knew they'd be doing more than that.

Eight

It felt good to take control of things again and not just drift, not just let life move her around as if she were a chess piece on some giant board. A pawn with no say in what was happening to her.

With each day that passed, Joanna felt a little stronger, a little more confident about herself as a mother, a little more confident about the direction her life was going to be taking.

At least in the practical sense.

She'd been to her gynecologist and gotten a clean bill of health. All systems were go, and her body had bounced back to where it had been nine months ago. She'd gone to see her home insurance agent—alone over Rick's protests—and filled out all the necessary paperwork in order to get the rebuilding on her house going.

She'd even been in contact with the head of the local school board.

That was where she had gone this afternoon, to see Amanda Raleigh, the head of the school board. Though she'd arrived at the local unified school district building with a considerable number of butterflies flapping madly in her stomach, the meeting had gone extremely well. Better than she'd anticipated. She hadn't had to wage a verbal war to get her old job back. Mrs. Raleigh had been very cordial, very accommodating. Not a bit like she'd been four months earlier when the woman had all but volunteered to sew a scarlet *A* on her dress.

But all that was behind her now. Two minutes into their meeting, Mrs. Raleigh had informed her that a position at a new high school would be waiting for her in the fall.

That just meant she had to get through the spring and summer somehow.

Joanna was already making plans. There were temporary agencies she could turn to during that time. Someone had to be able to make use of her abilities until she was teaching again in the fall.

All in all, she thought as she drove her car up the winding path to Rick's estate and into the garage, she was feeling pretty good about herself.

There was only one area that still resounded with question marks. An area that neither she nor Rick were willing or ready to broach.

Just where did they stand beyond the moment?

Before his parents had successfully conspired to pull them apart, she and Rick had been ready to face the future together for all time. With the confidence of the very young, they had made plans to get married in the spring.

Would that be in the future again? Would they get married? Would they even have a relationship once she left the confines of his estate?

She didn't know.

She did know that any thoughts about the future, other than the practical ones about providing for herself and Rachel, left her with an unsettled feeling. It was the same nervous feeling that had caused her to shy away from the myriad of men with whom her friends insisted on setting her up. Over the last few years, one of her friends was always touting someone "who's just right for you."

How many times had she heard that phrase? Too many to count.

But despite accolades to the contrary, the "someone" was never right. There was always some flaw that pushed her away before a second date could come about. Joanna knew damn well that she was probably not being fair to any of the men she'd gone out with, but she just couldn't help it.

Fear was a powerful deterring factor and while she thought herself fearless in so many aspects of life, she knew herself well enough to admit that she was afraid of getting hurt again.

So afraid that she didn't even want to venture into the field again.

So afraid that even now that her "perfect someone" had materialized in her life again, she didn't know if she had the courage to tread over the same terrain with her heart exposed to the elements.

It had been all she could do to pull herself together

the first time. The only reason she'd succeeded was because she'd had her mother to lean on. Rachel Prescott was the strongest, bravest person she knew. Her mother understood what it meant to pull yourself upright after love had all but disintegrated your heart. Though her mother had never once spoken ill of him, Joanna knew that her father had broken her mother's heart. He'd left her abruptly the moment he'd found out that she was pregnant, virtually disappearing from the scene.

Her grandfather, a strict disciplinarian, had thrown her mother out because she'd refused both of his ultimatums: abort her baby or give it up for adoption when it was born.

Her mother had been all about love, and because of her, because of her unwavering support, Joanna had found her own courage to go on after she had left Rick and he had left town.

Without her mother in her life, Joanna didn't know if she could do it a second time, if she could recover if things didn't go right. Under the circumstances, it was best not to test her at this point in her life. Her own daughter needed her and the baby came first.

The bottom line was that she couldn't allow her heart to go there, couldn't let herself dream and hope. She refused to live beyond the moment when it came to Rick.

Getting out of her car, she noticed that the Mercedes was parked beside the Mustang. Rick was home.

Once, when he'd had her over while his parents were away in Europe, the garage had been filled to capacity with his father's collection of automobiles.

His father had always loved displays that touted his wealth, his importance.

The collection was all but gone now. Three of the vehicles had found their way to Florida, his father's other residence, and two were still here for when he lived on the west coast, but for the most part, the car collection had been given to charity. That, she knew, had been Rick's doing. She'd heard from Mrs. Rutledge that Howard Masters now believed that there were more important things than money.

Would wonders never cease?

Too bad he hadn't felt that way eight years ago.

She closed her door, looking at her own small foreign car. Rick had had it brought over last week. It looked completely out of place here amid the other cars. Like a poor relation allowed to eat at the table because it was Christmas.

Kind of the way she probably would have felt if she'd married Rick, she thought.

She supposed she could see his parents' side of it, why they had balked at having a daughter-in-law whose parents hadn't even bothered to get married, much less been able to have their lineage traced back through noble bloodlines.

The years had brought her insight she fervently wished she didn't have.

In the absolute sense, his parents were right. Rick had a great future before him. He needed "his own kind" as his mother had put it, beside him, not someone who was a bastard in the old sense of the word. A man should be proud of his wife, not embarrassed by her.

And that was what she would have been to him. An embarrassment.

"Did you run into a problem?"

The sound of Rick's voice coming from the entrance to the garage startled her. Joanna turned around. The sun was behind him, framing him in golden rays as if he were the Chosen One.

She couldn't help smiling. Maybe he was at that, she thought.

The Chosen One, but not chosen for her. He'd assumed the helm of his family's business with ease. And in that time, he'd only become better-looking. She'd thought of him as beautiful to start with, but the years had tempered that beauty with a ruggedness that was almost irresistible. She couldn't help wondering why he wasn't married by now. What had happened to the woman his mother had chosen for him? The one she'd stepped aside for?

Didn't matter. That wasn't her concern. She banked down her thoughts and responded to his question. "No, why?"

"I heard the car." Crossing to her, he nodded at her vehicle. "When you didn't come in, I thought maybe something was wrong. You were frowning."

She dismissed his observation. "Just thinking."

Taking her chin in his hand, he tilted back her head. His eyes searched hers for a clue. She'd become a great deal more closed-mouth than she'd been when they had been together. "About?"

"Thoughts. And to answer your question, nothing's wrong. The school board told me that, after reviewing the matter, they're willing to have me come back."

She wasn't telling him anything he didn't already

know. He slipped his arm around her shoulders, beginning to usher her toward the house. "Very gracious of them. Maybe they don't like facing the possibility of a lawsuit."

She looked at him, puzzled. "Why would they think I'd sue them?"

There was a note in her voice that warned him to keep his part in this under wraps a while longer. "Everyone sues these days."

Joanna stopped walking and shrugged his arm away from her shoulders.

"Did you have something to do with this?" Now that she thought about it, Mrs. Raleigh had looked a little uneasy. All things considered, the woman had seemed a little too eager to reinstate her.

"I didn't talk to anyone there."

She knew him. He was being deliberately evasive, deliberately telling her small truths to fabricate a larger lie. He hadn't talked to anyone *there*, which meant that he *had* talked to someone somewhere about her situation.

Joanna felt her temper emerging. "Who *did* you talk to?"

Rick's shrug was charmingly noncommittal, but she was in no mood for charm. "I talk to a great many people every day."

He was playing games. She pinned him with specifics. "About me."

He waved his hand in the air, tossing her a diversion. "I asked Mrs. Rutledge—"

Joanna fisted her hands on her hips. "Rick!"

He wasn't about to lie outright to her. Besides, he wasn't ashamed of what he'd done. It was all very reasonable, all very aboveboard. It was the school district who had been in the wrong, not him. "I had my lawyer talk to them."

She should have known. Angry, she curbed the urge to slug him. Given his physique, he wouldn't have felt it and it might have even injured her knuckles. But that didn't negate the desire.

"Damn it, Rick, how could you?"

Why was she getting so angry? He tried to appeal to her logic. "Joanna, it's discrimination. In this day and age, an unmarried pregnant woman—"

"—can fight her own battles." Didn't he get it yet? His mother had been an independent woman. Did he think that was only a trait reserved for the rich? "*I* wanted to fight my own battles. Win my own battles." She blew out a breath. "Now I can't go back."

He didn't see the connection. "Why? Because I did what you were going to?"

How dense was he? Or was he just patronizing her? "Because you did it *for* me."

He studied her for a moment. "Since when did ego become such a big thing with you?"

It wasn't about ego. It was about self-esteem. Apparently he couldn't distinguish the difference between the two. "Since I wanted to be my own person." She wanted him to understand. She wasn't being ungrateful, she was being herself. She didn't want to lose that sense of self, not even for him. It carried too big a price.

Her voice softened a little as she told him, "I can't have someone else charging into battle for me, I can't start relying on that."

It didn't make any sense to him. "Why?"

She closed her eyes for a second, gathering strength together. He really didn't see, did he? She spelled it out for him.

"Because when you lean on something and that support suddenly crumbles, then what happens? You fall flat on your face. You fall hard enough and you're not going to get up again."

She was talking about herself, he realized. Funny, they'd grown apart, grown in different directions, and yet, they shared this. The fear of abandonment. He would have preferred being able to share something else.

"Not you, Joey." He tucked a strand of hair behind her ear, the way he used to do. And she shook it loose, the way she used to do. A smile curved his lips. "You always get up again. It's one of the things I liked about you." She'd been soft, but she'd never clung. She didn't need him to be strong constantly. But he found himself wanting her to need him a little. "I also liked the fact that you used to let me do things for you once in a while." He framed her face with his hands, trying to secure her complete attention. "People need to be needed, Joey, just as much as they need to feel invincible."

Placing her hands over his, she slowly removed them from her face. "I don't want to feel invincible, Rick, I just want to stand up on my own two feet."

"And you are." A touch of exasperation filled his voice. "I wasn't threatening the board, trying to make them take back a shoddy teacher, I was trying to make them see the error of their ways and take back a wonderful teacher." Couldn't she see the difference?

He was just saying that, she thought. That hadn't

been his reasoning then. People in high positions get accustomed to having their wishes obeyed without question.

"How do you know I'm a wonderful teacher?" she challenged. "You've never even heard me teach."

"Because you're a wonderful everything else." His gaze washed over her, making her feel warm all over. She felt herself losing the thread of the argument. "I figured why should teaching be any different?"

She wanted to remain angry, to make him understand, but it wasn't easy. "You're making it hard to argue."

His grin teased her. "That was my intent."

She had to make him understand why it was important to her. "But I want to argue. Don't you see—"

He slipped his hands around her waist. "Do you know, trite as it sounds, that you're beautiful when you're angry?"

She sighed, knowing she was tottering on the edge of defeat. "Rick—"

"Of course," he said philosophically, "you're beautiful when you're laughing so I suppose that's not much of an accomplishment."

The man was utterly impossible. And incredibly irresistible. She could feel the heat of his body traveling through hers. "Rick—"

He shook his head, then kissed her forehead. "Sorry, you're not going to make me apologize for doing what's right."

Backing away from him, she threw her hands up. "You've got to stop doing this, Rick. Stop buying me things, being my bully—"

"Bully?" Now there was something no one had ever called him before. He paused, pretending to roll the image over in his mind. "I've never thought of myself as a bully. I'm more of the Sir Lancelot type, don't you think?"

If he was the first knight of the realm, where did he see her in all this? "And I'm Guinevere?"

He smiled into her eyes, drawing her to him again. "Yes."

But she shook her head. "I don't want to be Guinevere, the romance ended very badly."

He thought it over for a second. "Well, you're too pretty to be Merlin and if you're King Arthur, that takes this relationship into a whole other realm that I'm not prepared even to consider." For a moment, they were back in the past, sitting on her mother's porch, fantasizing. He grinned at her. "Okay, who would you like to be?"

"Me, Rick," she insisted, and then her voice softened. "Just me."

He nodded. "A very good choice. I vote for that, too." His hand around her waist, he began to usher her toward the inner garage door. "Now come into the house, I have something for you."

She sighed, exasperated. "Aren't you listening? I just told you I don't want you spending any more money on me."

"I swear, you are the hardest woman to shower with things. But don't worry, this didn't cost anything." For good measure, he crossed his heart, the way he used to.

It was like experiencing déjà vu. She shut the feeling and its accompanying sensations of nostalgia away. "You stole it?" she scoffed.

He thought of the box in his room. "No, I unearthed it." He opened the door leading into the house and waited for her to walk in first.

Now he had her curious. But first, she wanted to look in on her daughter. She'd discovered that being away from Rachel for more than a couple of hours at a time filled her with a sense of longing. It was going to be difficult once she went back to work—one aspect of independence she wasn't looking forward to.

"Let me just go in and check on Rachel first before you start 'showering.'"

He laughed. "Why don't we do it together? See the baby I mean, not shower—although—"

This time she did hit him, but she laughed as she did it. "You know, this isn't over with yet."

"I sincerely hope not." There was a look in his eyes that completely unsettled her.

She looked at him pointedly. "I mean this discussion."

Mrs. Rutledge came out to greet them the moment they entered the house. Her proximity to the inner door had allowed her to hear almost everything.

"I was beginning to wonder if I was supposed to bring out the swords for you two." She was referring to the two ancient samurai swords that hung over the fireplace in the den. "And a referee." She looked at Joanna. "Did everything go all right at your meeting with the school board?"

Joanna in turn slanted a look toward Rick. "That depends on who you ask." She supposed, in his defense, from Rick's point of view, he was only trying to help. A lot of women would have killed to have someone in their corner. The problem was, he wasn't in her corner, he *was* the corner.

"You'll work it out," Mrs. Rutledge assured her with unflagging cheerfulness. She saw the two begin to go toward the rear of the house. "I just put the baby down. Mind you don't wake her."

Joanna shook her head as the woman walked away. "I'm starting to wonder whose baby this is," she murmured to Rick.

"She tends to be a little protective," he told her, and then added as he looked at Joanna, "There's a lot of that going around."

Tiptoeing into the nursery, Joanna saw that Rachel really was asleep. She'd been hoping to find her awake. But she didn't have the heart to rouse her.

Standing here, looking down at her daughter, raw emotions found her. She was still in awe of the fact that she was a mother, that this tiny life had entered hers and that she was responsible for it.

It both humbled her and filled her with a great deal of love.

"She looks like you."

She felt his breath along her cheek as he spoke and struggled not to shiver. "No, she doesn't."

Maybe she'd misunderstood what he meant. "When you were a baby."

Drawing away from the crib so as not to wake Rachel, she looked at him. "How would you know?"

"I sat up last night, looking through your mother's albums." He nodded toward the open door, indicating that they should take the conversation out of the room in case it might wake the baby.

"Why would you do that?"

"I was just curious." He eased the door closed and followed her into the hallway. "You're not seriously going to turn the board down because of your pride, are you?"

"My pride?" Stunned, she looked at him. "What does my pride have to do with it?"

"Everything from where I'm standing. For some reason, you feel as if you have to do everything yourself. The world's not like that, Joanna."

She'd watched her mother struggle to provide a living for them. There'd never been anyone to help her and she'd never complained. It was just something she did and it was a trait she'd passed on to her.

"It is for me."

He shook his head. "The world is about networking, about doing favors and having them done for you. You're being noble in your own way, but you're also being damn stubborn in a way that only you can be."

She frowned. "What's that supposed to mean?"

But he only grinned at her. "That's okay, I like stubborn women." He kissed her temple. "Now come with me." He took her hand, threading his fingers through hers. "I still have something to show you."

Nine

The moment he started walking with her toward the staircase, his cell phone rang.

Joanna looked at his jacket. "I think your pocket wants you."

Rick sighed, stopping. He wasn't in the mood for interruptions. "I'm going to have to remember to turn that off when I come home."

"There's always the regular phone," she pointed out. One of the rooms served as his office. "Your fax, e-mail. They'd find you."

She was right. There was no getting away from responsibility. He hoped that this was something that could be settled quickly. Pulling out his phone, he saw that Joanna was about to walk away, probably to give him some privacy. He held up his finger, indicating that he wanted her to stay.

"Masters."

Joanna watched his face as he listened to the person on the other end of the phone. His brows slowly drew together like dark clouds gathering before a storm. "Can't you handle it, Pierce?"

Whoever Pierce was, Joanna thought, his answer was obviously negative. Rick's eyebrows almost touched over the bridge of a nose that sculptors had been immortalizing for centuries.

"Fine, I'll be there in twenty minutes." Annoyed, he slapped the lid shut. He was frowning deeply as he replaced his phone in his pocket. The frown faded slightly as he apologized. "I'm going to have to go out for a little while."

From what she'd seen of him these last few weeks, she wouldn't have expected anything less. He was in full command of the company, not just his father's right-hand man. That meant that business would take up most of his time. She was surprised that he could come home early. "A man's gotta do what a man's gotta do."

He ran his hands up and down her arms, his eyes on her face. "What this man wants to do is spend the evening with you." Impulse had him forming plans as he went along. It had been a long time since he'd felt spontaneous within the confines of his own life. "I wanted to take you out and celebrate your rehiring. You haven't been out since Rachel was born."

If only he knew. "Far longer than that," Joanna laughed.

There was something in her voice that made him want to ask her questions, made him want to find out what life had been like for her these years they'd been apart. Had there been anyone else after him? Someone who'd captured her heart? What other men had held her? Had made love with her?

Or had she been like him, alone in her heart if not in reality?

He knew he had no right to ask, but that didn't change the fact that he wanted to. That he wanted to know.

Taking her hands in his, Rick looked into her eyes, losing himself there for just a moment.

"I won't be long," he promised. "When I come back, we'll go out. Does dinner and dancing sound good to you?"

Joanna grinned. "Right now, a hamburger and a jig sound good to me." *Any place,* she thought, *as long as it's with you.*

"It'll be more than that. Maybe this'll hold you until then. Take it as a retainer."

Rick meant only to brush a fleeting kiss to her lips, nothing more. He didn't have time for more. Pierce, his chief assistant, brought with him from Georgia, sounded harried. It looked as if one of the divisions of Masters Enterprises might have a wildcat strike on their hands.

But touching his mouth to hers only made Rick want to kiss her again. Life had a way of wantonly turning things inside out without giving any notice. He knew that now. Gathering her into his arms, he kissed her as if he wasn't coming back. As if she wouldn't be here when he did. As if the world was going to end in the next five seconds and all they had available to them were these precious few moments.

He was draining away her soul. As he drew his lips

back, Joanna had to hold onto his arms just to steady herself. If she'd been an old-fashioned galleon, she would have sworn that she had just been broadsided and breached.

Still holding on to his arms, she pretended to shake her head to clear it. It was only half in jest. "Wow, if that's a retainer, I can't wait to find out what the whole payment is."

He brushed the back of his hand against her cheek, a bittersweet feeling filtering through him. All the warnings he'd issued to himself were temporarily on hold. He just wanted to enjoy the sight of her. "Just be ready when I come back."

"I'm not sure if that's possible," she murmured as he left the house. She was beginning to think that nothing would prepare her for him, not at this level of intensity.

She couldn't help wondering if he'd forgotten all about that mysterious "something" he'd alluded to earlier. She knew she'd told him to stop giving her things, but he'd made her curious.

Passing a mirror, she grinned at her reflection. Rick still had the ability to make her feel as if she were no more than twenty.

Rick unconsciously tightened his hands around the steering wheel as he took a turn. It took effort to make himself relax and loosen his grip. He glanced at the clock on the dashboard. Eleven-oh-two. He had to work hard to rein in his anger and curb it.

The quick meeting had been anything but that. It definitely hadn't gone as planned. What should have taken no more than an hour had stretched out into

four, then five, threatening to go well into the pre-
dawn morning until he'd finally called a halt to it,
promising to reconvene the next day.

Obviously he wasn't as on top of things as he'd
originally thought, otherwise the workers at the Pas-
adena plant would not be threatening to walk if certain terms were not met.

When it rained, it poured. As if his life wasn't hec-
tic enough with the home office transfer, he was now
in the middle of a work arbitration.

The meeting felt as if it were a million miles away.
Right now, all he was concerned about was finding a
way to make it up to Joanna. He didn't want her to
feel that he was taking her for granted, that he expected her to stand on the sidelines, waiting until he
could spare a moment for her.

He'd called her twice from the office, pushing back
the time until there wasn't any time to push back.

He felt really awful. There weren't enough hours
in the day, but somehow, he intended to find them.
Or create them if he had to. There had to be a way
to be a conscientious businessman while still main-
taining some kind of a private life. He hadn't wanted
one up until now, but things had changed, at least
temporarily. He needed to find a way to be able to
juggle both, he thought, getting out of the car.

It was after eleven. Too late to eat out. And probably too late to make it up to Joanna. The evening
wasn't supposed to have gone this way.

Feeling drained and annoyed, Rick let himself in
through the garage.

"So, how did it go?"

Glancing toward the living room, he saw her getting up from the sofa. She was wearing a robe and her hair was slightly tousled, as if she'd just been lying down.

He closed the door behind himself. "You waited up for me?"

She shrugged carelessly. The sash on her robe loosened slightly, the two sides parting a little. "I waited. I'm up, so I guess you'd be safe in saying that I waited up for you."

Crossing to her, he flashed an apologetic smile as he slipped off his jacket. This time, he'd made sure his cell phone was off. He dropped his jacket on the back of the sofa. "I'm sorry about tonight."

"Why, did it go badly?"

Her makeup was gone, and she looked as natural as sunshine. He could feel himself being aroused. "No, I meant about us not going out."

"Well, unless there's some kind of edict about closing down all the restaurants in the world by tomorrow morning, I figure you can make it up to me." There were still frown lines about his mouth and eyes. She feathered her fingers along his brow, pressing them away. "Did you get a chance to eat?"

He nodded, loosening his tie then slipping it off. It joined his jacket. "We sent out for sandwiches. How about you?"

"I got the better end of the deal." She threaded her arms around his. "I had Mrs. Rutledge." The woman had insisted on making her a full dinner. "There's some leftover beef Wellington in the refrigerator if you're interested." She waited to see if he wanted her to warm up a portion for him.

"Beef Wellington?" It was one of Mrs. Rutledge's

specialties. "You really did get the better end of the deal."

As far as food went, anyway, she thought. The evening had gone very peacefully. Rachel had been perfect company, sleeping for most of it. "Sometimes things turn out that way. So, are you hungry?"

"Yes." But as she turned to go to the kitchen to prepare a late meal for him, he caught her by the wrist and pulled her back. When she turned to look at him quizzically, he said, "I'm hungry, but it doesn't have anything to do with food."

"Oh?" She cocked her head, looking up at him. "What does it have to do with?"

Instead of saying anything, he pulled her closer to him and brought his mouth down on hers. The kiss began passionately and ended practically in flames.

By the time he drew his mouth from hers, they were both breathing hard.

"That," he told her.

She threaded her arms around his neck. Her eyes danced with mischief as she looked up at him. "Aren't you too tired for 'that'?"

He locked his hands behind her, his pulse beginning to accelerate. "Did it feel as if I was tired?"

She sighed, wishing the moment and this feeling would go on forever. Knowing it couldn't. "It felt like heaven."

He glanced toward the rear of the house, where the nursery was. "When was the baby fed last?"

"Twenty minutes ago."

One down. "And Mrs. Rutledge?"

Tongue in cheek, she said, "She ate about three hours ago."

He pressed a kiss to her throat, then another. Her pulse leaped up to mark the passage of his lips. "I meant is she asleep?"

"She said good-night at ten." It was hard to get the words out when her head was spinning.

"That's all I wanted to know."

His lips found their way back to hers again. He kissed her hard, the way he had earlier before he'd gone to his meeting. The way he'd wanted to all evening.

Joanna could feel her blood rushing in her veins as her whole body went on alert.

It wasn't going to end here, in the hall, with a kiss that curled her toes so hard she might never be able to straighten them again.

This was just the beginning.

Anticipation sang through her body, priming it. Making her ache so badly, she almost whimpered. Joanna wrapped her arms around him even tighter, raising herself up on her toes. Trying to absorb every nuance of his kiss, every nuance of his body. To sustain her later.

It wasn't easy, but he pulled his head back to look at her. "You sure it's okay?" he breathed.

It was more than okay, it was wonderful. The grin on her lips came into her eyes as she looked at him. "Well, if we make love out here, Mrs. Rutledge might see us if she wakes up and hears something."

He laughed, kissing her quickly before saying, "You know what I mean."

It touched her that he was so concerned about her well-being at a time like this. Another man would be ripping her clothes off by now. Independence not withstanding, it was nice to have someone worry about her, even if only fleetingly.

"Yes, I know what you mean." She brushed a kiss to each of his cheeks. "And the doctor said I'm fully operational."

The description made him laugh. "That makes you sound like an aircraft."

Her arms around his neck, she pressed her body tantalizingly against his, swaying just enough to make him crazy. Her eyes never left his as she said seductively, "Come fly me."

It was all he needed to hear.

The instant he kissed her again, needs that had been held back for so long broke free of their chains. He kissed her over and over again, changing the chemical composition of her body from solid to almost completely liquid. Heated liquid.

And then, it seemed as if her body was on automatic pilot. Her arms still around his neck, she jumped up, wrapping her legs around his hips and waist. Her mouth never broke contact with his.

He caught her, holding her to him. She could feel her inner core moisten and yet seem to be on fire. Her mouth slanted over his again and again.

All the years of longing pushed forward, fueling her desire, beating against her with fisted hands as they begged to be finally freed.

She was playing havoc with his restraint, bending it all out of shape until he didn't know how much longer he could contain himself. He could feel the inner heat emerging from her, hitting him square in the stomach, whetting his appetite and raising it to incredible heights. His mouth sealed to hers, his consciousness all but disintegrated, he was barely aware of walking with her.

Somehow, they made it into her room, though the logistics of how didn't completely register. All Joanna was aware of was the overwhelming desire that had taken her body hostage.

How many times had she dreamed about this, digging deep into her memory and reconstructing every time they'd been together? The first time, the last time, they'd all merged into one compelling memory, making her long so much that it hardly seemed humanly possible to feel this way and still live.

But she'd managed. Managed to survive for a long time without him. Without anyone.

But now that was at an end. She was going to make love with him tonight. She had to. Otherwise, she was going to self-destruct.

Joanna felt as if there were explosions going on all over her body.

Slowly, he drew her away from his body and laid her down on her bed. Her robe parted. The nightgown she had on exposed more than it covered. His mouth became as dry as the Mojave in summer.

As he lay down next to her, he could feel his entire body pulse to a rhythm that had been set down before time was recorded.

He tugged her robe from her shoulders. Joanna raised her hips to accommodate him and he felt in danger of swallowing his tongue as he pulled the robe off the rest of the way. The silken material slid unnoticed to the floor.

Covering her mouth with his, Rick took his assault to two fronts, his lips reducing her to the consistency of tapioca pudding left out overnight while his hands delved beneath her nightgown, finding places that had existed only in his dreams. Places that had once been his.

Joanna drew her breath in sharply against his mouth as she felt his fingers spread out over her hip, caressing her softly over and over again. Regaining possession. She turned into his touch, savoring it, then abruptly pulled away.

When he looked at her in confusion, she breathed, "No fair."

Before the words could penetrate the growing haze around his brain, before he could ask her what she meant, Joanna began making short work of the clothes he was wearing.

Understanding, he leaned back and quickly undid the buttons of his shirt.

But she was the one who pulled the tails out of his waistband, the one who pushed the shirt off his shoulders as she craned her neck in order to capture his mouth with her own.

The next to go were his pants. Wiggling almost beneath him, she undid the button, then the zipper, her hand delving inside the space that was created to touch him lightly before she continued removing his pants.

He moved to help her, but she was clearly in charge. A woman with a mission. "You've done this before," he teased.

He could have sworn there was a twinkle in her eyes. "I've practiced on mannequins."

He didn't want her to think that he was prying. She had the right to be her own person, the right to her privacy. As much as he wanted to know, he wouldn't ask. He wanted her to know that.

"I'm not asking about your past, Joey."

"There is no past, Rick." Hot with her breath, the words echoed against his mouth. Unable to rein in her emotions, she yanked away his underwear. "There's only you."

He didn't know if she meant that, if there'd been no man in her life since they'd separated. But true or not, he wanted to believe it.

So, for now, he did.

The flame within him raised ever higher.

Pressing her back against the soft comforter, he began to make slow, methodical love to every inch of her, beginning at her toes and working his way up as she twisted and sighed beneath him.

He lingered over every part of her, satisfying his own ever-increasing desire with the sounds and movements she made as he pressed kisses to her instep, to the back of her knees, to the insides of her thighs. Cataloging dusky tastes in his brain.

Remembering.

Finding the very heart of her, his tongue teased her, bringing her up to her first climax.

Joanna grasped fistfuls of the comforter, scrambling closer to the sensation that was exploding within her as his mouth branded her. Making her completely his, as she always had been.

She bit down hard on her lower lip to keep from crying out.

Panting, she fell back, only to be quickly brought up to the promise of a second explosion.

She reached for him, wanting to touch him, to possess him as he did her, but he was merciless in his quest to bring her pleasure.

He kissed her belly, making it quiver, weaving the chain so that it descended again before he finally took it upward.

He anointed each of her breasts, hardening the peaks until she thought she would go insane. And then, he was over her, poised, ready, wanting.

She realized that her eyes had been squeezed shut. She opened them now and looked up into his face. The face of the man she had always loved.

Framing it with her hands, she raised her head and pressed her lips against his. The kiss that flowered between them was velvety and deep.

It cut through the last of his resolve. He'd wanted to prolong the moment, to kiss and tease her a little longer before he finally came to her. But there was no way he could physically hold back even a moment longer. She'd weakened him, weakened him with the look in her eyes, with the soft promise of her body as it yielded itself up to his.

Uttering a sound that was only marginally intelligible, Rick drove himself into her.

His eyes holding hers, he began to move, at first slowly, then more and more rapidly with each beat of his heart. He'd wanted to watch her, to take in every movement, every tiny glimmer of her expression.

But the need to kiss her, to savor her lips, was even greater. Just as his body was sealed to hers, he sealed his mouth over hers.

As their hips moved and the tempo increased, so

did the urgency of his kiss until both erupted in one final, all-surrounding crescendo.

Within the small eternity that followed, Rick found the spark, the ecstasy, the peace that had been eluding him for so long. He clung to it.

Ten

Nestled in the crook of his arm, she'd been quiet for a while now. Rick wondered if that was a good thing. Brushing a kiss against the top of her head, he asked, "What are you thinking?"

He could feel her smile as it spread against his chest. The warm feeling following in its wake was indescribable.

"That you must have been practicing." She looked up, her hair brushing against his skin. "I don't remember you being this good."

He laughed softly. "I was always this good." The smile faded slightly as he looked into her eyes. "And I haven't been practicing."

He watched as her smile turned into a grin. "Oh, then you're telling me you've lived like a monk all these years?"

"Of the highest order." Rick winked and then crossed his heart with his free hand. "Want to see my membership card?" He pretended to reach for it, then stopped. "Oh, sorry, this outfit doesn't come with pockets." When she laughed, another warm feeling curled through his belly, like smoke from a chimney on a crisp winter morning. His arm tightened around her as emotions he'd been so certain had left him for good filled his heart. "I've missed you, Joey."

She turned into him, the humor gone from her eyes. "Why didn't you come after me?" There was no recrimination in her voice. She just wanted to know. "I was in the same place I always was. Why did you just leave town like that?"

He shrugged. Looking back, he knew he shouldn't have. He should have laid siege to her house until the truth came out. "Pride, I guess." He lowered his gaze to take her in. "The same pride that keeps you stubbornly fighting off help at every turn."

She shook her head, her hair moving along his arm. Arousing him again. "Apples and oranges."

"Fruit salad," he countered.

She stared at him in confusion. "What?"

The grin began in his eyes, filtering down to his lips slowly. "I thought as long as we're lobbing fruit around, we can make a salad."

Laughing, Joanna swatted at his arm. "You're talking crazy."

"Right." He fitted her against him, his eyes intent. "Then shut me up, Joey. I don't want to talk about the past." He kissed the swell above her breasts and felt her begin to shift, "or anything else, except that

I've got a very beautiful naked woman in my arms and I've remained inactive far too long.''

She could feel his desire for her growing. The man was incredible. ''Again?''

The look on his face was pure innocence. ''Hey, being a monk lets you store up an incredible amount of energy, lady…'' Suddenly, he whipped her around, making her land flat on her back. ''I have only begun to make love.'' He raised and lowered his brows comically. ''Think you're up to it?''

Her heart was already beginning to race. ''Why don't you try me and see?''

He shifted so that his body covered hers. ''Exactly what I had in mind.''

It wasn't until nearly an hour later that she found her tongue again. She had all the energy of a de-stuffed rag doll. As if he wasn't already perfect enough, the man was an incredible lover.

With what she thought was her last ounce of strength, she turned her body toward his. It amazed her that he hadn't fallen asleep yet. She splayed her hand against his chest, finding infinite comfort in the feel of his heart beating beneath her palm.

''By the way, was that a ploy?''

''What?'' He raised his head just a tad to look at her expression. ''That I can make love all night under the right conditions?''

''No, that you had something for me.'' She pushed herself up onto her elbow and her eyes sparkled as they dipped low on his torso. ''Or was that 'it'?''

''A little more respect, please,'' he teased, stealing a kiss. ''And no, 'that,' as you so irreverently called it, wasn't 'it.'''

Her curiosity was roused all over again, despite her resolve not to accept another material thing from him. "Then what?"

He laughed, drawing her closer. "Getting mercenary on me, are you?"

"No," she protested with just enough indignity to have him guessing whether or not she was serious. "I just want to know when you're feeding me lines."

"I'd never feed you a line." Sitting up, he threw off the sheet and got out of bed. "Wait here."

She bolted upright. "Rick, you can't go out like that. What if Mrs. Rutledge sees you? She'll have a heart attack."

"I wasn't about to go parading up the stairs in my birthday suit." Rick grabbed his pants from the floor where they'd been discarded and put them on quickly. Pulling up the zipper, he didn't bother buttoning them. "Wait here."

"With bated breath."

Moving the pillows against the headboard, Joanna sank back against the bed, sighing. She felt exhausted, excited, energized all at the same time. All that and in love as well.

She knew she shouldn't be, that it was a mistake to fall in love with Rick all over again. She knew that what his parents had said was ultimately true. She and Rick belonged in totally different worlds. A temporarily out-of-work love child with next to no roots and a multi-millionaire with bloodlines that went back to the Thirteen Colonies had little in common. They could hardly be mentioned in the same sentence.

But for now, for tonight, Joanna thought, lacing her fingers behind her head, she could let the practical

world go and just pretend that she was still just
Joanna Prescott, twenty years old and wildly in love.

Because she was.

She glanced toward the doorway. Rick had returned
and he was carrying a rectangular, unwrapped, white
shirt box in his hands.

Unlacing her hands, she made herself comfortable.
"That was fast. Grabbed the first thing you could find,
did you?"

"No." But he had grabbed the first box he could
find in order to make it look like a gift. Rick sat down
on the bed next to her. "I grabbed the gift I had for
you. The one I was going to give you before Pierce
called in the middle of his heart attack." She looked
at him uncertainly. "Figuratively speaking. Pierce is
always having heart attacks. He enjoys being dra-
matic."

He put the box on her lap. As she moved forward,
the sheet began to slip from her breasts and she made
a grab for it. He stayed her hand.

"No, don't. Let it fall." He moved her hand away
from the sheet. "Let me have my fantasy."

She raised an amused brow. "Your fantasy is
drooping sheets?"

"No," he pressed a kiss to her shoulder and had
the pleasure of feeling her shiver ever so slightly,
"my fantasy is you." He nodded toward the box on
her lap. "Well, aren't you going to open it?"

She caught her lower lip between her teeth, looking
down at the box.

"Let me savor this. Sometimes, anticipation is the
best part." And then she looked at him. His hair was
still tousled where she'd run her fingers through it.

Joanna could feel her skin glowing just thinking about what they'd done. "Except for tonight," she said softly.

He curbed the temptation to run his hand along her breasts, reveling in the softness of her skin. Instead, he nodded at his gift. He wanted to see her face when she opened it more than he wanted to fulfill his erotic fantasies. "The box."

"The box." Joanna placed her hands on either side of the gift. "And you're sure this didn't cost anything?"

"Not a dime," he assured her, just the slightest bit impatient. "Even the box was one that was just lying around."

A grin played along her lips. "But you think I'll like this."

She was messing with him and she knew it. "Open it already. Here," he reached for the box, ready to open it for her himself, but she pulled it aside.

"No," she laughed, "I can open my own free gifts."

And then, as the lid came off and she held it in her hands, the laughter stilled.

There was an album inside. Its cover had been weathered slightly by the passage of time. She recognized it as one she'd given him years ago. She'd always thought he'd thrown it away.

Joanna said nothing as she carefully took the album out of the box and set it down on her lap. Then, very slowly, she lifted the cover and looked inside. There was page after page of photographs. The photographs that she'd lost in the fire. Tears filled her eyes.

"It's not free," she whispered, "it's priceless. But where did you get this?"

"From my closet. From deep in my closet," he added. "I couldn't make myself get rid of it." The album had been there all these years. He hadn't taken it with him when he'd left town, hadn't wanted to look at anything that reminded him of her.

She still didn't understand. "I thought you said you didn't care about keeping photographs, that you didn't need them."

Inside the album was every single photograph she'd insisted on giving him. Each time she'd had a roll of film developed, she'd made duplicates of all the shots that contained the two of them. And each and every time, he'd acted cavalierly, claiming he didn't believe in keeping photographs, even after she'd given him the album as a keepsake.

Rick shrugged. The truth was, he was far more sentimental than he'd ever wanted to admit.

"Saving photographs didn't sound macho. A twenty-two-year-old guy wasn't supposed to get sentimental over something like that. These are all the ones you lost in the fire." Craning his neck, he looked at her. "You're crying." A shaky sigh escaped as she nodded. Taking a corner of the sheet, he wiped away her tears. "Happy tears?" She nodded again. Rick shook his head. "That never made any sense to me. It's like *aloha* and *shalom,* words that can mean two completely opposite things."

Emotion welled up inside her. She carefully placed the album on the nightstand and then turned back to Rick. Wrapping her arms around his neck, she hugged him as hard as she could. "Thank you."

He kissed the top of her head, not trusting his voice at the moment. The heat of her body began working its magic again. He could feel himself becoming aroused just holding her.

He glanced over toward the nursery. ''Think Rachel'll sleep a little longer?''

''She's been sleeping longer and longer these days.'' Mentally, Joanna crossed her fingers. ''I think Mrs. Rutledge's been training her.''

He could just barely remember what the woman had been like when he was growing up. Strict, but kind. ''God bless Mrs. Rutledge.''

She watched unabashedly as he rose and slid his pants from his hips. ''What did you have in mind?''

Rick got into bed with her. ''Round three.''

She wiped the last of her tears away with the back of her hand, having absolutely no idea how much that aroused him. ''Ready when you are.''

''Ready,'' he declared.

Rick pulled her back down on the bed. He lost no time revisiting places he had gotten far more familiar with in this short space of time than he was with his own body.

Weaving a wreath of hot, open-mouth kisses along her quivering skin, he paused only long enough to say, ''When it comes to you, Joey, I was born ready.''

''Big talk,'' she teased, arching her body temptingly against his, savoring the burst of desire that erupted within her each time his mouth made contact. ''Actions speak louder than words.''

''Then prepare to go deaf.''

Taking her hands, he held them above her head, locking his fingers through hers. His body was less than a hairbreadth away from hers, tantalizing her, making her yearn for the coupling she knew was to come. He moved against her just enough to make her crazy.

Joanna felt herself growing damp, could feel the throbbing need in her own loins. Two could play this game, she thought. She arched against him, then gloried in the smoky look that came into his eyes.

With one slow, teasing movement of her body, the warden had become the prisoner, the captor had become the captured.

She held him in the palm of her hand. He knew that in some ways, she always would. How had he lived so long without this woman, without feeling her supple body yielding itself to his? How had he been able to withstand the days without losing himself within her?

Containing himself as best he could, holding both her hands in one of his, Rick moved down the length of her, branding her with his lips, his tongue.

He was creating havoc within her very core. Joanna could feel the precursors of climaxes reaching up to greater and greater heights within her, wanting the final moment, the final triumph. And just when the climax threatened to erupt, he'd pull back just enough to keep the moment from happening.

It was torture, and she loved it.

Finally releasing her hands, he framed her body, lightly skimming his fingers along her skin even as his mouth reduced her to the consistency of quivering warm jelly.

"You're making me crazy." The words came in short, breathless spurts.

''Good,'' he murmured against the tender flesh of her stomach, his warm breath arousing her to almost a frenzy.

She bucked beneath him. ''Now, Rick, now.''

He wasn't sure if it was a plea or an order. Whatever the case, it came because she wanted him as much as he wanted her. And it came at the right moment because he knew he couldn't hold out much longer.

Pulling himself up along her body, her dampness exciting him, he stopped just short of entry. Poised over her, his eyes held hers for a long moment.

She felt as if time had suddenly been frozen.

There was so much she felt, so much she wanted to say. So much she couldn't say.

But he could read it in her eyes.

There was no need to part her legs, she was ready for him. Eager for him. He drove himself in, his breath catching in his throat from the start.

And then the dance began, not a waltz, but a wild tango, heated from the very start, pledged to get only more so before the music stopped.

The final explosion came quickly, draining them both. He held her in his arms as tranquillity descended, wishing that this moment *could* somehow be pressed within the pages of time, to be revisited, refelt, whenever he needed to remember what it was like to love someone so much that nothing else mattered.

He kissed her temple. ''Loud enough for you?''

Joanna moved her head so she could look at him. ''Eh? What did you say? I can't hear you, I've gone temporarily deaf.''

He laughed and hugged her to him. And felt himself getting aroused all over again.

The woman was more than part witch, he thought. And she was all his.

The rest of the night was spent in further exploration, in testing the limits both of their endurance and the boundaries of their creativity.

He found himself doing things with her that had never even crossed his mind, found himself assuming positions that would have made a yoga master proud. And while she had always been an exciting lover, the years of deprivation had transformed her into an aggressive one.

More than once, she assumed the lead, making him the one who wanted to sit up and beg.

For mercy.

For more.

She teased his body, tempting it, tantalizing it, bringing it up almost to a climax and then knowing just how to retreat in order to heighten the experience when it finally came.

He was in complete awe of her.

In complete awe of his own body and how it responded to her.

And somewhere in the night, amid lovemaking and dozing, heat and contentment, all the doubts that had been plaguing him slipped silently away.

It was almost idyllic. As close to paradise as she would ever get, living or dead, Joanna mused at the end of the following week.

But on some level, she kept waiting for it to end.

For the serpent to make his entrance and cause her ultimate banishment.

Life was almost too perfect.

She had a wonderful new daughter, someone to help her out when she stumbled—the way her mother would have, had she lived—and a man she adored who came home to her every night. It was so much more than she'd ever had before.

Rachel had learned to sleep through the night, allowing her not to if she so chose. Since that first night together, she and Rick made love every night. The nights belonged to both of them, and the past as well as the present.

But with each day that passed, the thought that she had to be getting out on her own grew a little stronger, made itself known a little more. She couldn't keep putting it off, not if she wanted to keep her own self-respect. And that was as important to her as he was.

What cinched her resolve even more was the fund-raiser he took her to in the middle of the week. It was an annual affair to raise money for one of his mother's favorite charities. Rick felt obligated to make an appearance and he asked her to come with him. Against her better judgment, she agreed.

His friends, the people who inhabited the world his parents had so carefully crafted for him years ago, welcomed him back to Southern California with opened arms. Their arms, however, were closed when it came to Joanna. They left less than an hour after they'd arrived.

"You don't have to leave on my account," she told him, hurrying beside him as he strode out the door after a woman had nodded toward her and asked him if he was slumming. "Stay with your friends."

"I'm leaving on my account and those are not my friends. Those are just people I used to know. People," he told her firmly, "I don't want to know anymore. Not if they can't be civil to you."

All she could think of that night, as he made love with her and tried to make her forget the misspent hour and the unthinking comments aimed in her direction, was that his parents had been right after all. She didn't belong in his world.

That Friday, Rick came home early, full of plans for the two days that lay ahead. He wanted to take her to Catalina for the weekend, to make up for the fund-raiser. He knew that night still bothered her and he wanted to erase it from her life.

Rachel was old enough to be separated from her mother for a couple of days. The weather promised to be idyllic, and he'd personally booked passage and made hotel reservations on the island.

In an incredibly good mood, he came in the front door looking for her. She wasn't in the living room, but he found signs that she'd been there. The classified section was spread out on the coffee table.

Rick stopped to look at it. His smile faded. "Joanna?"

"In here," she called from the kitchen. When he came in, he was surprised to see her in an apron, surrounded by pots. There was something boiling on the stove. "You're home too early. I'm making dinner tonight and I just started." She stopped when she saw the look on his face. "What's wrong?"

"What's this?" Rick dropped the newspapers he'd found on the kitchen table. The page was turned to the rental section and there were several listings circled in bright red.

She shrugged casually as she reached for flour and spread it out on a plate. She'd told him when she came that she didn't intend to stay here permanently. "Apartments for rent."

He struggled to contain his anger. "Why are you looking for an apartment?"

"To move into," she replied. Joanna dusted the flour from her hands. "The check came from the insurance company today."

He frowned. "I thought you said you were rebuilding the house."

"I am." She took out a plate of chicken cutlets she'd prepared earlier. Closing the refrigerator, she placed the plate on the counter and began coating each piece with the flour mixture. "This check is for living expenses. I had a rider on the policy that if something happened to the house and I couldn't live in it for a while, the policy provided funds to allow me to rent a place while reconstruction was taking place." Turning away from him, she opened the cabinets and rummaged around for a suitable frying pan.

Rick placed himself in front of her. "Is this because of the fund-raiser? Because of what Alyssa Taylor said?"

"No," she said firmly. "This has nothing to do with Alyssa."

"Aren't you happy here?"

Taking the frying pan out, she put it on the stove.

"It's not a matter of being happy, Rick. It's a matter of taking charge of my life."

"Independence again."

She could hear him huff the word out behind her. Annoyed, she turned around and looked at him. Why was he so determined not to allow her to stand on her own two feet? Did he want her to be a clinging vine? "Yes, independence again."

He didn't care for her tone. "I haven't exactly kept you chained in the basement."

She sighed. She didn't want to lose her temper. He'd been good to her. More than good. But this was just something she needed to do. The fund-raiser had only reminded her.

"You haven't kept me chained at all. You've been wonderful." She went back to preparing the meal. "But I told you, I can't let myself get used to this."

He took the knife out of her hand and held her arms still. "Why?" He searched her face for an answer. "Why can't you let yourself get used to it?"

"Because this is *your* house."

"It could be yours, too."

A soft smile curved her lips as she shook her head, denying his assertion. "I don't think squatters' rights apply to mansions, Rick."

At times, she could be the most exasperating woman. "I'm not talking about squatters' rights. I'm talking about spouse's rights." He saw her eyes grow huge and moved in for the kill. "Marry me, Joanna."

It took effort not to let her jaw drop. "Just like that?"

"No, not just like that. We'll need a license, blood tests, a priest—"

She pulled her arms away from him and moved back. "Stop kidding around."

"I'm not kidding around. I'm serious." He turned her around again to look at him, then took her hands in his, half imploring, half trying to keep the edge out of his voice. "Marry me, Joanna. You, me, Rachel, Mrs. Rutledge, we'll be a family."

She wasn't buying it, wouldn't allow herself to buy it, not for one moment. He was trying to make up for what she'd endured. "I won't have your pity."

It wasn't easy hanging onto his temper. "There's nothing about pity in the marriage vows. They've even taken out the word *obey*."

Why was he making this so hard for her? Didn't he understand? What they had was wonderful, but it couldn't be permanent.

"Rick, your parents were right. I hated them for it, but they were right," she insisted, her voice nearly breaking. She refused to allow herself to cry. "I'm just a teacher, an out-of-work one at that until the fall. You're a jet-setting multi-millionaire." He was still being dense, she could see it by the look on his face. "I'm a mutt, you're a pedigree. People are going to keep reminding you of that."

Was that it? Was she afraid of what people like the ones at the fund-raiser would say? To hell with that. To hell with all of them. Didn't she know that?

"The kind of people who'd remind me of that are the kind of people I don't want to associate with," he insisted. As she tried to pull away, he held her wrists fast. "And as for 'pedigree,' I don't want to try to create thoroughbreds or show dogs, Joanna, I want to create a marriage. I thought you did, too."

This was breaking her heart. He had to see that, she thought.

"I'm not in your league," she insisted, knowing that eventually, the matter would come up. She needed to say it before he did. Before he resented her for all the things she wasn't.

"What 'league'?" he cried, his temper dangerously close to erupting. "We're not playing baseball here. I'm trying to forge a good life for myself. And you're part of that life. I lost you once because I was too stubborn to block out my pride and come after you. I'm sure as hell not about to let your pride keep us apart."

Joanna sighed. "Then maybe I'd better leave now so that you can see this clearly—"

"Damn it, Joanna, you're the one not seeing things clearly. You're the prejudiced one, not the insufferable, egotistical people you think will stand and wag their fingers in my face for having the good sense to fall in love with someone who's—"

He stopped abruptly when he saw the look on Joanna's face. She was looking toward the doorway. "We're not alone."

He swung around to see Mrs. Rutledge standing there. Her expression was unreadable. "Mr. Rick, there's someone to see you."

He wasn't in the mood for anyone. "Mrs. Rutledge, I'm in the middle of a hell of an argument right now." He waved dismissively, turning away from the housekeeper. "Tell whoever it is to come to the office on Monday."

"I don't plan to come to the office anymore, unless I'm invited, of course."

The familiar voice had Rick pulling up short. Stunned, he turned around again and saw that, as incredible as it was, he was right.

His father was standing directly behind Mrs. Rutledge in the doorway.

Eleven

Rick moved forward, putting himself between his father and Joanna.

He seemed oblivious to the protective gesture, but it wasn't lost on Joanna.

"Is this about the potential wildcat strike? Because if it is, that's over."

"Yes, I hear you handled that quite nicely. No, this isn't about the wildcat strike. I'm not here to look over your shoulder anymore."

"What are you doing here, Dad?"

Tall, gray-haired and just gaunt enough to be still referred to as suave, Howard Masters gave his surroundings a short once-over before answering. "Well, unless I miss my guess, until a short while ago, I used to live here."

Apparently her timing was excellent, Joanna

thought. She'd started looking for a place to rent just in time. "Are you moving back?"

Rick's father turned his gray-blue eyes in her direction. It was impossible to know what he was thinking, but the look in his eyes appeared kindly. "Would that be an inconvenience?"

"Not at all, sir." To make her point, Joanna picked up the newspaper from the table and folded the page she wanted, slipping it into the pocket of the apron as she looked at Rick.

There was a ghost of a smile on his father's lips. "Hire a new cook, Richard?"

Damn it, the old man knew what Joanna looked like. He took instant offense for her. "No, Dad," Rick said tersely, "this is—"

But Howard cut in deftly, his lips curving into a full-fledged smile as he looked at her. He inclined his head in a silent show of respect.

"Joanna Prescott, yes, I know. I was only teasing, son. I haven't had much practice at it, so I imagine it didn't come across that way. Perhaps my field is more in the area of deadpanning," he proposed, then gave a small half shrug. "At least, that's what Dorothy says." He looked from one to the other. "From the sound of it, I was interrupting something."

Joanna got back to her work. "Nothing that won't keep, Mr. Masters."

"Call me Howard. I've decided to become less formal in my remaining years." The announcement was met with stunned silence.

Obviously unmindful that he appeared completely out of his element, Howard wandered over to the large pot simmering on the stove. Three sets of eyes watched him with more than a little wonder.

Lifting a lid, he inhaled deeply. "Am I correct in assuming that you're making dinner?"

Was he toying with her for some reason? Should she be bracing herself for some kind of mind-blowing confrontation? "Yes."

He carefully replaced the lid before turning toward her. "May I stay?"

She was just thankful there were no gusts of wind traveling through the house, otherwise she was certain she would have been blown flat on her face. It took her a second to recover. "As you pointed out, Mr. Masters, it's your house."

It wasn't the answer he was after. "May I stay?" he repeated, waiting. His tone gave every indication that the question was genuine and not meant to bait her.

Joanna exchanged looks with Rick. He didn't appear to know what was going on any more than she did. "Yes, of course."

Enough was enough. If his father was playing some elaborate game to embarrass Joanna, it wasn't going to happen, not while he was here to stop him. "Dad, what's going on?"

Rather than take offense at the sharply voiced question, Howard looked at his only son affably. "Part of my new lease on life, Richard. I'm not taking anything for granted anymore." He looked at Joanna. "Do I have time to freshen up?"

He certainly looked like the man who'd tried to buy her off eight years ago, but he definitely didn't sound like him. "Dinner won't be ready for an hour."

Howard nodded, pleased. "Splendid. I'll see you in the dining room then." As he walked out of the kitchen and past Mrs. Rutledge, he gave her a nod of approval. "You're looking very good these days, Nadine."

"Thank you, sir." The words dribbled from her lips. Mrs. Rutledge's eyes shifted to Rick, silently questioning him. But he merely lifted his shoulders in a confused shrug.

"Positively eerie," Mrs. Rutledge murmured to herself after the senior Masters left the room. In all the years she had worked for the man, this was the first personal comment, much less compliment, that he had ever given her. Giving her head a quick shake to clear it, she turned to Joanna. "So, tell me, how may I help?"

It seemed odd to have a woman so capable in the kitchen willingly take a back seat and assume the role of assistant. But she had no time to waste arguing about who belonged at the helm here. Joanna glanced toward the end of the counter. "The potatoes need peeling."

Mrs. Rutledge went to wash her hands. "Consider them peeled."

"And what about me?" Rick asked. There was an edge in his voice. He still wasn't entirely convinced that his father was here purely for altruistic reasons, that he wasn't here to somehow sabotage his life, the way he had eight years ago. "What role did you have planned for me in all this?"

The comment about too many cooks spoiling the broth played across her mind. She went to find a colander. "You can play the part of the hungry but patient lord of the manor."

He knew how to read between the lines. "Which means get out of your way."

Joanna looked at him over her shoulder, grinning for the first time since he'd walked into the house. "Exactly."

She was using this as a respite from what they'd been talking about. She knew that he wasn't about to try to argue with her while Mrs. Rutledge was in the room and his father could walk in on them at any time. This was a private matter just between the two of them. Okay, he'd table it for now. He might be wounded, but he was by no means defeated. His mistake eight years ago was in not pushing. A man learned from his mistakes.

He leaned over her and whispered in her ear, "To be continued."

"I never doubted it," she murmured under her breath as he walked out. Putting the matter out of her mind for the time being, she looked over toward Mrs. Rutledge. "Thank you."

Long, spiral peels piled up beside the cutting board as Mrs. Rutledge made short work of the potatoes before her. She raised only her eyes as she continued peeling. "For what, dear?"

She knew that the woman was on top of everything, had heard everything. "For not asking questions."

"Not my place, dear," Mrs. Rutledge responded blithely.

But that was what it was about exactly, Joanna thought. Place. And hers was not beside Rick.

* * *

Howard Masters entered the dining room and took his place at the head of the table just as Joanna put down the last of the covered dishes on the table. He noted that there were only two places set.

He looked at her. "You're not joining us?"

Joanna avoided Rick's eyes. He'd asked her the same question less than a minute earlier. She'd just assumed that his father wouldn't want her at the table and after turning Rick's proposal down, she was in no mood to be placed in a position where she might be belittled.

She took a step toward the doorway. "Well, no. I thought that you two would want to eat alone."

"No, please," Howard countered, "join us." He looked at his housekeeper who had brought in the main course, chicken parmesan. "Mrs. Rutledge, please bring another place setting for the young lady." Before Joanna could protest, Howard pulled out the chair to his left, directly opposite his son. "Please," he coaxed Joanna, "sit."

She had no choice but to do as he asked, allowing him to push in her chair for her.

Taking his own seat, Howard smiled at her. "I see that you've brought the settings closer together." He nodded his approval. "Much better." He turned toward Rick. "Your mother and I always wound up shouting whenever we ate in here." Raising his wineglass to his lips, he took a long sip before setting it down. "Of course, that seemed to be the natural order of things. I suspect we would have wound up shouting even sitting as closcly as this." He turned his attention to the dishes before him, helping himself to a sizable serving of everything on the table. "Everything looks very good, Joanna. I had no idea you were so capable."

This was a father Rick hardly recognized. He had half expected, after the confrontation they'd had over the telephone regarding the deception, that his father would reconnoiter and take the offensive again. This was completely unfamiliar territory for him. The heart attack really *had* changed him for the better.

Rick made an effort to clear things up and get back on stable footing. "You said something when you arrived about not going to the office anymore?"

"Yes." Howard paused to savor a piece of the chicken and then nodded his approval. "I've decided to retire. Officially. All my life, I believed that a man was defined by his family, his work. That ultimately meant having no identity of his own. No life of his own. At sixty-seven, I've decided it's high time I had one."

An identity, huh? Rick wasn't sure if he was buying into this new, improved model his father was purporting to be. "And just who are you, Dad?"

Howard's smile was stately, regal. Howard could see that his son didn't believe him. That was all right, there were times when he was surprised himself at this turn of events. Surprised and grateful for a second chance.

"I'm just discovering that, Richard. And the process, they tell me, is half the fun." He looked at Joanna. "Wouldn't you agree?"

Joanna felt as if she was shell-shocked. "Is that what you'd like me to do? Agree?"

"My dear young woman, I want you to do anything

you want to. Really." He knew that wasn't enough, that they weren't going to believe him, either of them, until he showed them how sincere he was. Laying down his knife and fork, Howard took a breath, bracing himself. "I suppose this has to be gotten out of the way before anything can move forward." He shifted slightly in his seat, looking at Joanna. "I apologize, Miss Prescott. I did you a great disservice eight years ago.

"I could, of course, blame it on Richard's mother. That would be the easy way out. Richard can testify that she was a very strong-willed, opinionated woman and she is gone, so she wouldn't be able to contradict anything I said." His smile was philosophical. "However, since I did not have my spine surgically removed, that isn't really an excuse. No one can make you do anything, and the truth is, at the time I thought that a marriage between the two of you would be a great mistake."

He saw that his son was about to interrupt. Holding his hand up, he quickly continued. "You must understand," he addressed his words to Joanna, "I come from a long line of blue bloods and snobs. We like to fancy ourselves a cut above everyone because, three hundred years ago, our ancestors had the good fortune to be sent to this country, crammed on a ship that was barely seaworthy. Never mind that they were most likely thieves and undesirables, the only creatures who came to the new world with a fair amount of regularity. They were forefathers and that was all that counted. Over the centuries, they were all whitewashed and elevated to a level just a little above saints and a half breath below God.

"What I am trying to say, in a very roundabout way, is that there *was* no excuse for doing what I did. Whatever my opinion regarding a proper spouse for my son," his smile was ironic, "lying, intimidating and forging should not have entered into it." He took Joanna's hand in his, strengthening his appeal. "I am truly sorry for what I did and can only hope that you will find it in your heart to someday forgive an old man his foolishness."

It took Joanna a moment to recover. The man had caught her completely off guard. And, as always, when confronted with an apology, any ill feelings she might have felt quickly disappeared.

Besides, she had already seen his side of it. Had made it known to Rick that she understood. "You were only doing what you thought was best for Rick."

Howard looked at his son. "I see what you see in her. Aside from beauty, she possesses compassion, a very rare quality indeed. It only makes me regret my actions more."

Joanna had never been the kind of person who enjoyed turning the knife in someone's heart. "There's no sense in harboring regrets about the past, you can't do anything about it."

"Other than learn from it," Howard agreed. "And I have. Life is too precious to waste dragging your feet or putting off anything that needs doing." He gazed at his son pointedly. "That's why I came here. To make my apology to you in person and to tell you that I am bowing out of the picture."

Howard raised his wineglass in a toast. "Masters Enterprises is all yours, Richard. Other than my stock options and the annual shareholder's vote, I am divorcing myself from the company entirely. Putting myself out to pasture, so to speak.''

His father had alluded to this during their last call, but Rick had been certain it was just a passing thought, soon to be glossed over and forgotten. ''I don't know what to say.''

Howard placed his glass on the table. ''Good luck comes to mind.''

''Of course.'' Try as he might, despite the last few months, Rick couldn't see his father in the role of a man on a permanent holiday. He'd always felt that his father *needed* to work. ''But aren't you being too hasty? The company was always your life.''

''And isn't that a sad thing?'' Howard eyed his glass, shaking his head. ''Dorothy taught me that,'' he confided to Joanna. ''The legacy we leave behind is not a building, but deeds, people we've touched as we pass through life. People who are better off because we've passed their way.'' His sadness melted into a smile as he reacted to her expression. ''Ah, you're beaming. You agree with me.''

''With my whole heart.'' He had just espoused her own philosophy. She couldn't have been more surprised.

''Snap her up, Richard, or I might decide to beat you to it.''

Rick was still trying to come to terms with what seemed to be his father's epiphany. ''What would Dorothy say?''

Howard laughed. ''Dorothy Wynters is a wild, free soul who doesn't want to get married. She says she's happy enough just 'keeping company.''' His tone dropped to one of confidentiality. "But I hope to change her mind soon." He reached into his pocket and took out a black ring box. Opening it, he held it so that Joanna could get a good look at its contents. "What do you think?"

She'd never cared that much for jewelry, but the ring, a three-carat heart-shaped blue diamond, took her breath away. "I think I should have worn my sunglasses." She grinned. "That has to be the biggest diamond I've ever seen."

Howard closed the box, returning it to his pocket. "Could a woman say no to this?"

"It would be hard," Joanna allowed. It seemed odd to her that the man was asking her reassurance. Never in a million years would she have ever imagined herself in the scene she was now in. "But coupled with you, I don't see how."

Howard laughed. The sound surprised her. Joanna distinctly heard an echo of the laugh she loved so dearly. Rick's laugh was a carbon copy of his father's.

"Charming, too. You are an incredible package, Miss Prescott."

The man was actually likable when he gave himself half a chance, she thought. "Joanna, please."

Going through the motions of eating, hardly tasting his food at all, Rick could only stare at his father. "Who *are* you?"

"As I've told you, I'm in the middle of discovering just that," Howard said.

As far as she was concerned, Rick's father had already found that out and was on his way to building a better life. "So, do you have a date in mind?"

"Any date she says yes to." Howard finished his

meal and leaned back with the rest of his wine.
"You'll both come to the wedding, I trust."

"Absolutely." Joanna's enthusiasm was solitary.
She slanted a look at Rick, raising her brow at his
glaring silence.

Rick held his hands up, as if to slow down the
assault of the words that were coming, fast and furi-
ous, his way. He shook his head. "I'm still having
trouble absorbing all this. Just what kind of medica-
tion are you on, Dad?"

"The best. Love. I never thought it could happen
at my age. Hell, I never thought it could happen at
all." He paused, his eyes never leaving his son's face.
"You must know that your mother and I weren't exactly a love match. More like a merger of two old
families for the purpose of propagation." He shut his
eyes and shook his head. "When I think of all the
time that I've wasted—"

Howard opened his eyes when he felt a hand on
his.

Joanna was looking directly into the older man's
eyes. "No going back, remember? Just forward. Today is the first day of the rest of your life isn't just a
trite saying, it's also true."

He smiled his thanks.

Howard remained for another hour. Joanna intro-
duced him to her daughter when the infant woke from
her nap. She was completely straightforward about
the baby's conception.

Rick expected some sort of cryptic comment at the
very least. His father stunned him by commenting fa-
vorably on Joanna's strength of character.

"You go after what you want. I admire that in a

woman." After glancing at his watch, Howard rose to his feet. "Well, as much as I hate to cut this short, I have a flight to catch and these days, they're advising us to arrive at the airport hours ahead of time." He surrendered Rachel to Joanna. "I only came to California to see my lawyer about what needed to be done in order to transfer the company to you, Richard, and," he looked at Joanna, "to make amends if I could."

They walked him to the door, flanking him on either side. Turning to face them, Howard took Joanna's free hand in his. "I've done you a grave injustice, Joanna, and you've been far more gracious to me than I deserve. That said, I hope that Richard comes to his senses and brings you into the family before someone else takes it into his head to snap you up." He placed her hand on his son's. "You two belong together and I had no right to try to change that. I realize that now."

Touched, Joanna leaned forward, as Rachel made bubbles and gurgled against her chest, and brushed a kiss on Howard's cheek.

He looked at her, smiling. "You are a true lady." Then he turned toward his son and surprised him by embracing him. "Take care of her, Richard."

Feeling a little awkward, Rick returned the embrace. "I'd like to, but she won't let me."

His hand on the door, Howard paused and looked at Joanna. "What's this?"

Shifting Rachel to her other arm, she patted the baby's bottom. "I believe everyone should take care of themselves."

Howard frowned. "That's all well and good when

it comes to 401K retirement plans. Otherwise, a little interdependence never did anyone any harm.'' He leaned forward and pretended to confide to Joanna, ''And men like to feel that they're still necessary for something. Take pity on us.'' He glanced at his son, then back at her. ''Humor us and allow us to ride to the rescue once in a while.'' He winked at her, then embraced his son again. ''Thank you for your hospitality and your forgiveness. I'll be in touch.''

With that, he let himself out. Joanna stood staring at the closed door a moment before turning toward Rick. ''Who was that masked man?''

Rick could only shake his head. ''Damned if I know.''

Twelve

Rick waited patiently, keeping the subject under wraps while they bathed Rachel and got her ready for bed. But once the baby was asleep, he felt under no obligation to hold back any longer.

The moment Joanna emerged from the nursery, he said, "I'll have that discussion now."

Well, it wasn't as if she didn't know it was coming. Joanna pressed her lips together, searching for strength. Rick was making it harder and harder to stick to her guns. Having him right there beside her helping to care for Rachel went a long way to disintegrating a resolve that wasn't made of steel to begin with.

But the memory of the fund-raiser was still very vivid in her mind. It was that image she hung on to in order to help her remain steadfast on rather wobbly legs.

Walking past him, she went into her room. It wasn't going to be hers for much longer, she thought. "There's nothing to discuss."

He followed her, closing the door behind them. Mrs. Rutledge had said something about retiring for the night, but voices carried.

"Then you don't love me."

She swung around, wounded by his assumption. If her whole course of action was going to depend on making him believe she didn't love him, then it was doomed from the start because no matter how resolved she was not to ruin his life, she couldn't tell him she didn't love him. It just wasn't in her.

"I didn't say that."

"You didn't have to." He blew out a breath, struggling to hang onto a temper that was badly frayed. "When a woman turns down a man's proposal, that's usually some kind of indication that she's not all that crazy about him."

Didn't he understand? They weren't children anymore. How many ways did she have to say it? "Love doesn't conquer all, Rick, society does. And like it or not, you're smack-dab in the middle of the social world."

Incredulous, he shook his head. "I feel like I've stepped into some kind of time warp, or a parallel universe or something straight out of *Star Trek*. My father sounds like you and you sound like my father."

Any minute now, she was going to cry. For years, in the small, sad wee hours of the morning, she'd thought about what she'd done, about what they could have had together. Now he'd asked her to marry him and she'd had to turn him down. For his sake. And it was killing her.

"Some things you just can't buck. Wasn't going to that party enough for you?" she cried. "I didn't even know what fork to use."

Rick stared at her, dumbfounded. "And that's it?" he demanded. "You're basing our entire future, the rest of our lives, on a fork?"

She threw her hands up. Why couldn't he just leave it alone? There was nowhere to go in her room, nowhere to escape. She went for the door. "You're twisting things."

He caught her by her arms and turned her around to face him. He wasn't about to let her run off.

"And I'll keep on twisting them until they're the way I want them to be. And no," he denied, one step ahead of her, "it's not about control, it's about happiness. And the shooting down thereof."

Releasing her, he dragged his hand through his hair, frustration chewing huge chunks out of him. "Damn it, Joanna, they have classes to teach you how to use a fork. They don't have classes to teach you to be you." He was shouting, he realized. With effort, he lowered his voice. "Stubborn but wonderful."

"I'm doing this for both of us." Her eyes pleaded with him to understand. He hated that. He wasn't going to benefit from having her refuse to be his wife, he was going to suffer because of it.

"And what my father said hasn't changed your mind?"

Life-altering epiphanies at his father's stage of the game didn't count. "He's lived his life. He has nothing to lose."

"And I do?" he shouted at her.

Rick didn't trust himself to keep a civil tongue in his head any longer. Abruptly, he turned on his heel and strode away from her.

Two minutes later, she heard the front door slam. The sound reverberated in her chest. Her first impulse was to run after him, to tell him she'd changed her mind. But she held herself fast. She couldn't allow herself to be weak. It was because she loved him that she was doing this and she had to remember that. So instead she sank down on her bed and remained in her room.

But God, it hurt.

She'd barely dropped off to sleep when she heard the knock on her door.

Immediately alert, her first thought was that something had happened to Rick. She'd spent most of the night pacing, praying. Waiting for him to come home. When he didn't, she'd thought of calling all the hospitals in the area to see if there'd been an accident.

By two o'clock she was beyond exhausted and had lain down on the bed, telling herself she needed to get some rest. After all, she was supposed to start apartment-hunting by nine.

Leaping out of bed, she ran to the door and swung it open, half expecting to see Mrs. Rutledge bearing some kind of dire news.

"What is it—?"

She nearly slammed into Rick.

Catching her balance, she stepped back, looking up at him. He was all right. Nothing had happened to him. Relief flooded through her.

The next second, anger caught up to her. How could he have put her through this? She hit his chest with the flat of her hand. "It's almost three o'clock in the morning. Where the hell have you been?"

He glanced down at the sheets of paper he had tucked against him. "Gathering evidence."

"Evidence?" Her eyes narrowed. "What are you talking about?"

Something his father had said earlier at dinner had triggered him. "I called my father at the airport and he gave me a list of names. I spent the rest of the time looking them up."

He'd completely lost her. And it was no excuse for storming out the way he had. "Names, what names? Rick what are you talking about?" She searched his face for telltale signs. "Have you been drinking?"

"No, but don't think I wasn't tempted." For the first ten minutes after he'd left the house, he'd seriously thought about doing just that, before a more productive course of action suggested itself. "But getting drunk wasn't going to solve my problem."

He was talking in circles, circles she wasn't following. "What problem?"

"You." Taking the conversation out of the hallway, Rick strode into her room and dropped the pages he was carrying on her bed. They fell like so many autumn leaves on top of her rumpled sheets. "Read that." He gestured toward the pages. "Pick any order you want to, it doesn't matter."

She looked at the pages. "What is that?"

Rick laughed shortly. "Those are my illustrious ancestors." Since she didn't look as if she was going to pick a page up, he did. He took the first one from the top. "Oh, here's a good one. Simon Greeley, born 1657 or thereabouts. Cutpurse." He looked up at her. "In case you don't know what that is, it's exactly what it sounds like. Someone who cuts the strings off your purse. In other words, a thief. Simon comes from my mother's side." He couldn't help grinning, thinking how aghast his mother would have been to know that there was someone like Greeley lurking in her family tree. "I'm sure she would have been thrilled to know that."

Discarding that one, he picked up another sheet. "Here's another one of my mother's people. Jenny Wheelwright. Street prostitute. No date of birth but she was shipped to Georgia in lieu of a death sentence in 1689." Tossing the page aside, he chose a third sheet. "Here's one of my father's glorious forebears, Jonathan Masters, common thief." He grinned broadly. "Notice the emphasis on the word *common?*" He began to reach for another. "There's more. Would you like me to go on?"

She didn't get it. Why was he deliberately berating his ancestors? "What are you doing?"

"I thought that was obvious. Showing you my bloodlines. After all, you've got a right to know what you're getting into. This—" he gestured at all the sheets littering her bed "—is my family.

"Oh, and in case you're interested, I also took the liberty of finding a few of Alyssa Taylor's relatives and a couple for some of the other people who attended the fund-raiser. Not one of them have clans that could exactly be called pure as the driven snow," he assured her. "And then I did you."

She stared at him. "Me?"

He nodded, sitting down on the bed. He began pulling the pages together into one pile again. "Took a little time. I only had your mother's name to work with. Since you've never told me it, getting your father's name was a little tricky."

Where was all this coming from? And why had he gone to all this trouble in the middle of the night? "How—?"

"Hospital records," he answered simply. "His name is on your birth certificate."

She knew that couldn't have been readily available to him. There was only one way he could have gotten the information. "Since when did you become a hacker?"

"I'm not, but my assistant is loaded with a lot of hidden talents. Most are parlor tricks, but this one turns out to be very handy. When it comes to extracting computer files, Pierce is a veritable Houdini. I worked him to death tonight and left him facedown on his bed. But I digress," he told her, and he became serious. "According to my information, you're the best one of all of us. Not a single thief, murderer or strolling lady of the evening in your family tree. Just a lot of good old-fashioned honest laborers and farmers." He shifted around on the bed so that he could take her hand. "Maybe I'm the one who should be worried about you being ashamed of me."

Joanna stared at the sheets of paper on the bed. "You did all this for me?"

Tugging on her hand, he made her sit down beside him. ''Well, you're the one who needs convincing, not me. I already know that you're the best thing ever to happen to me. And, if anyone ever makes you feel the slightest bit out of place, I'll just give them a peek at their family tree and I guarantee that you won't get a second haughty look out of them.''

Joanna shook her head. This had to be the sweetest thing anyone had ever done for her. ''I don't know what to say.''

He cupped her cheek. ''I believe the operative word of the day is still *yes.* As in, 'Yes I'll marry you.' 'Yes, I'll go to Catalina with you—'''

This was coming out of left field. ''Catalina?''

In the excitement of his father's unexpected visit, he hadn't had a chance to tell her. ''I booked tickets for us to go tomorrow—today,'' he corrected. ''Oh, and yes, I've also got something for you.''

She wasn't sure if she could take anything more. But before she could ask him what else he had up his sleeve, Rick took out a velvet box from his pocket and handed it to her.

She opened it and immediately recognized the ring. There couldn't possibly be two like that. She looked up at him, puzzled. ''This is your father's ring.'' Joanna tried to give it back to him.

He pushed her hand gently back, closing her fingers around the box. ''No,'' he corrected, ''technically, it was to be Dorothy's ring.''

She still didn't understand. ''Then how did you get it?''

His father had slipped it into his pocket when he'd

embraced him at the door. The show of emotion had completely caught him off guard.

"He gave it to me just before he left, saying that he saw the way you looked at it and thought it might help me convince you." Rick searched her face. "Was he right?"

Didn't he know her yet? "I wouldn't marry you just because of a ring."

He knew that. The ring was just to sweeten the deal, a token to symbolize his affection. "Would you marry me just because you love me? Just because I love you?" And then he grinned. "And just because I won't give you any peace until you do?"

"You know they call that stalking, don't you?" It wasn't easy keeping a straight face. Or keeping herself from throwing her arms around his neck.

"They used to call it determination." Rising to his feet, he took her into his arms. "I don't care about labels, Joey. Or what 'society' says. I care about you, about your baby. About the kind of life we can have together. And the kind of life I'd have without you." He looked into her eyes. "I've already seen it and I don't like it. I had to keep myself busy twenty-four hours a day just not to think about you. And most of the time, it didn't work. Remember, you were the one who once told me that the most important thing in life is not what you do, but who you love and who loves you back." His arms tightened around her. "The most important part of my life is that I love you. And you've already told me that you love me. In my book, when people feel like that, they get married."

She no longer had the will or the energy to resist. "You're sure about this?"

"How many ways do I have to say it?"

She glanced over her shoulder at the pages on her bed. She laughed. "You've already found plenty of ways to say it."

"Now I only want you to say one thing."

She lifted her chin, struggling not to laugh. "One thing."

He nipped her lower lip. "Wise guy."

Her smile faded as she became serious. "Not so wise. I walked away from you once."

"And now?"

"I'm not walking anymore." *Ever again,* she promised silently.

Rick nodded, pleased. "Good, then I'll cancel the work order to put bars and deadbolts on all the windows and doors."

She laughed. "It wouldn't have gone with the style of the house anyway."

It was his turn to grow serious. "The only thing that I care about going with the house is you."

"Okay."

But he shook his head. The glib answer wasn't enough. "I want to hear this formally. Joanna Prescott, will you do me the supreme honor of becoming my wife?"

She could feel her heart swelling with love. "Yes, oh yes." Throwing her arms around his neck, she kissed him.

Just as the kiss flowered with the promise of passion, they could hear the sound of the baby crying over the baby monitor. Joanna drew back reluctantly. "My baby's crying, I'd better go to her."

"Our baby's crying," he corrected. "And we'll both go to her. In a minute."

He kissed her again, long and hard, just to seal the bargain.

* * * * *

If you enjoyed
A BACHELOR AND A BABY,
you'll love the third book in
Marie Ferrarella's
exciting four-book miniseries:
THE MOM SQUAD
The third book will be available in May 2003
from Silhouette Intimate Moments:

THE BABY MISSION

Don't miss it!

Don't miss the latest miniseries from award-winning author Marie Ferrarella:

The MOM SQUAD

Meet...

Sherry Campbell—ambitious newswoman who makes headlines when a handsome billionaire arrives to sweep her off her feet...and shepherd her new son into the world!

A BILLIONAIRE AND A BABY, SE#1528, available March 2003

Joanna Prescott—Nine months after her visit to the sperm bank, her old love rescues her from a burning house—then delivers her baby....

A BACHELOR AND A BABY, SD#1503, available April 2003

Chris "C.J." Jones—FBI agent, expectant mother and always on the case. When the baby comes, will her irresistible partner be by her side?

THE BABY MISSION, IM#1220, available May 2003

Lori O'Neill—A forbidden attraction blows down this pregnant Lamaze teacher's tough-woman facade and makes her consider the love of a lifetime!

BEAUTY AND THE BABY, SR#1668, available June 2003

The Mom Squad—these single mothers-to-be are ready for labor...and true love!

Silhouette®

Where love comes alive™

If you enjoyed what you just read,
then we've got an offer you can't resist!

Take 2 bestselling
love stories FREE!

Plus get a FREE surprise gift!

Clip this page and mail it to Silhouette Reader Service™

IN U.S.A.
3010 Walden Ave.
P.O. Box 1867
Buffalo, N.Y. 14240-1867

IN CANADA
P.O. Box 609
Fort Erie, Ontario
L2A 5X3

YES! Please send me 2 free Silhouette Desire® novels and my free surprise gift. After receiving them, if I don't wish to receive anymore, I can return the shipping statement marked cancel. If I don't cancel, I will receive 6 brand-new novels every month, before they're available in stores! In the U.S.A., bill me at the bargain price of $3.57 plus 25¢ shipping and handling per book and applicable sales tax, if any*. In Canada, bill me at the bargain price of $4.24 plus 25¢ shipping and handling per book and applicable taxes**. That's the complete price and a savings of at least 10% off the cover prices—what a great deal! I understand that accepting the 2 free books and gift places me under no obligation ever to buy any books. I can always return a shipment and cancel at any time. Even if I never buy another book from Silhouette, the 2 free books and gift are mine to keep forever.

225 SDN DNUP
326 SDN DNUQ

Name	(PLEASE PRINT)	
Address	Apt.#	
City	State/Prov.	Zip/Postal Code

* Terms and prices subject to change without notice. Sales tax applicable in N.Y.
** Canadian residents will be charged applicable provincial taxes and GST.
All orders subject to approval. Offer limited to one per household and not valid to current Silhouette Desire® subscribers.
® are registered trademarks of Harlequin Books S.A., used under license.

DES02

©1998 Harlequin Enterprises Limited

The secret is out!

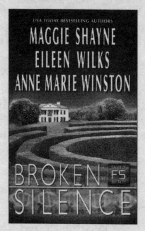

Coming in May 2003 to SILHOUETTE BOOKS

Evidence has finally surfaced that a covert team of scientists successfully completed experiments in genetic manipulation.

The extraordinary individuals created by these experiments could be anyone, living anywhere, even right next door....

Enjoy these three brand-new FAMILY SECRETS stories and watch as dark pasts are exposed and passion burns through the night!

The Invisible Virgin by Maggie Shayne
A Matter of Duty by Eileen Wilks
Inviting Trouble by Anne Marie Winston

Five extraordinary siblings. One dangerous past.

Where love comes alive™

PSBS

COMING NEXT MONTH

SDCNM0403